The Bad Love Trajectory

A Collection of Cautionary Tales

Glyn K Green

The Bad Love Trajectory

Published by Showborough Books

Copyright © Glyn K Green

Showborough Books
Showborough House
Twyning
Gloucestershire
GL20 6DN

www.showboroughbooks.com

CONTENTS

OEDIPUS GUY

It wasn't until Guy started school that he began to notice that he had at least fifty per cent fewer parents than a lot of children. Not all children, but enough to suggest to an observant small boy that the trend seemed to be for parents to come in pairs. With the odd set of four. And some variation. Mary McArthur, for instance, had two mummies living in her house and Philby had two daddies, and Janey Ritter had a different daddy every month, which was exciting in its way but not without its tensions.

At five years old, Guy couldn't analyse tension but he could feel it. And just as he recognised that some parents were appallingly rude to each other and some moodily silent, and others never together at all if they could possibly help it, he also recognised that he and his mother had the perfect arrangement: sunny, constant and exclusive. And always ready to accommodate whatever he wanted to do.

Guy's mother, Laura, had loved his father, but five years heals wounds and now she remembered him mostly as a charming, short-lived husband—a fast driver who, at the conception of his first child, had had the foresight to take out an enormous life insurance. Now, at twenty-eight years old and with Guy in school all day, Laura was ready to move on. Look at a career. Fall in love again. She didn't think that she and her son had the perfect arrangement. It was wonderful in its way but a woman has needs over and above those that can be met by a five-year-old child. Laura was ready to accept a man into her life. Guy, of course, was not.

This became evident the moment Mike Chalmers arrived at the front door. Not to Mike Chalmers maybe, or even to Laura, who welcomed him with newly washed, flowing blonde hair and a pretty print dress, kissed Guy goodbye a little distractedly - entirely overlooking that they were at a critical point in the bedtime book - and left him with Grandma, who was willing enough to read but no good at voices or elaborating on the bits that the author had carelessly glossed over. Such as, did superheroes always wear boots because they'd never learned to tie shoelaces?

"Who's that man?" Guy asked, brows drawn together, bottom lip prominently displayed.

"A friend of Mummy's," replied Grandma, pushing back his floppy hair.

Guy ducked sulkily. He knew all of his mother's friends and he was certain that she'd never had a big one like this, with a slick suit, a confident air and a wolfish smile. The man had predator written all over him. Guy didn't think in these terms, of course, except for the word "wolf" which sprang into his mind immediately, but he felt it all very strongly. And it spoilt his bedtime story and made him moody with Grandma, even though she let him come back downstairs and watch a DVD because it was Friday night.

He was still only half-asleep when his mother returned home at about ten thirty and came upstairs to check on him. As she bent over to kiss his brow Guy noticed immediately that she smelt differently. Hotter, muskier, stronger. A change that both fascinated and repelled him. A change that he knew instinctively had something to do with *that* man. He lay very still and kept his eyes tightly shut. He wanted his other mother. The one who smelt of chips and gardens and the dog.

Down in the hall, Grandma was already in her coat but before she left she had things to say. In her special hushed voice that was never hushed enough.

"You be careful," she warned Laura. "It's a long time since you've been in this situation. Times have moved on. Men are, well …" She hinted at new pinnacles of darkness and depravity in a tone that was not for one moment lost on Guy, who was now peering through the banisters.

"Mike's just popped in for coffee," said Laura. "This is not a planned seduction."

But Grandma knew all about men and their premeditated spontaneity. "That's what you think, Little Red Riding Hood," she said.

So this man was a wolf, thought Guy with his powerful, five-year-old certainty.

When Grandma had gone Laura went back into the sitting room and closed the door.

Guy strained to hear the mumbled conversation but all

3

he could catch were his mother's frequent little laughs. Small, helpless things they sounded. Anxious, placatory, stillborn. Guy's concept of the laughs was merely instinctive but he understood that they were nothing like the giggles and belly laughs his mother shared with him, and he viewed them with a direct and simple perception.

He listened for a while longer and then went back into his bedroom, opened his toy box and got out a big, red fire engine made of metal. Then he crept downstairs and approached the sitting room via the dining room in circuitous guerrilla fashion. The lights were dim, and now there was soft music which covered the noise of squeaking doors. Guy raised his eyes above the arm of the sofa.

The man was lying on top of his mother, squeezing all the life out of her, smothering her. His tie was off, his shirt was half undone and thick, black hair ran up from his chest to meet bristly, emergent stubble on his chin. His lips were drawn back in a wolfish grin, teeth just a flash of gleaming canines, and his tongue, raspberry pink, was obviously much too long to stay in his own mouth … "All the better to eat you with, my dear …" Guy grasped the fire engine firmly and brought it crashing down.

"*What the hell?*" The wolf leapt to his feet in a single great bound, holding his head and shooting furious glances around the room. Guy had retreated behind an armchair but the wolf spied him in a second - and took in the fire engine still clutched in his hands. "Why, you poisonous little puppy!" he yelled, in a choking voice.

Guy stood rooted to the spot looking incredulous.

Never, ever, had anyone spoken to him in such a way. For a while he was struck dumb, blue eyes filling with tears, and then he screamed, "*Shut up, you!* You horrid man. You were trying to eat my mummy."

"What's that he said?" asked the wolf of Laura who, so far, had been too busy zipping up her dress to intervene.

"You horrid wolf creature," Guy screamed again, just to make things clearer.

"He wants his bottom smacked," said Mike Chalmers. "The little beast. My head's actually bleeding." He looked at his red fingers.

"Beast yourself!" yelled Guy, dancing with rage in his bare feet. "Beast yourself. Horrid wolf beast." And he flung the fire engine with all his strength.

Before Laura could get hold of the situation the wolf beast crossed the hearthrug in one giant stride, seized Guy by the arm and fetched him an enormous one across the bottom. For a brief moment there was a horrified silence, and then Guy opened his mouth and bawled like an abandoned calf.

Laura had her arms round him in a second.

Over his wailing head she shouted, "Don't you *ever* touch my child again. In fact, don't you ever come here again. Get out!"

"But, Laura ..." Mike Chalmers tried to calm her. Draw her attention to his bloodstains. Apologise.

"Get out," said Laura.

When Guy had settled she gave him some milk and took him up to bed. With the wolf beast vanquished, he

5

soon started to feel quite talkative and began to explain how Grandma had muffed the bedtime story. But his mother didn't seem as interested as she should have done. They hadn't been "just playing" at all, Guy thought. The wolf beast had shocked her.

Grandma wasn't shocked. She always expected these things. "It's just like lions," she explained the next day. "When a new male takes over the pride he goes round killing all the cubs so that he can start afresh with his own. I saw it on David Attenborough."

*****

For six months after that there were no more men. No more wolves at the door. Then one Friday evening Guy came home from school, escorted by Grandma, to find his mother in the kitchen, hair in rollers, preparing the sort of food they never ate. The red lettuce and heaps of fresh herbs were interesting to him but not immediately threatening. He had more important things on his mind, such as how, that evening, his mother and he were actually going to eat fish fingers, followed by the new *Shrek* DVD that his friend Rutherford had just seen, and the next day they were going to the park with a picnic, then to the funfair which had just set up on the green.

"We can do all of that tomorrow, darling," said Laura absently, "but tonight …"

Guy found himself in bed at seven o'clock with the dawning suspicion that his mother was starting to smell different again. At eight, he heard the doorbell and a new voice. Low and growly. Ten minutes later he crept downstairs with his teddy.

The kitchen door was open so he went right in. There was a man leaning on the breakfast bar. Not the wolf man - not as big and dark - but smoking. In an intimate way and as close as it was possible to get to someone who was tossing a salad.

"My mummy doesn't like smoking," said Guy, in his high clear voice.

The man swung round in surprise.

"She says it tastes the food," Guy added.

The man raised his eyebrows and looked at Laura.

"In restaurants," she said hastily. "When there used to be a lot of it. Now come along, Guy, you're supposed to be in bed. Sorry about this, Paul."

The man took a long, satisfied drag on his cigarette and blew smoke at the ceiling.

"I don't like you," Guy said to him. "You're going to make Mummy's red lettuce taste of smoke and you're going to eat her."

"What?" The man looked at Laura again. "What's he say? Eat you?" He said this with a lingering smile which Guy found extremely unpleasant.

"He saw a bit of *Silence of the Lambs*," said Laura, quickly. "At his friend's house. Very careless of the parents. Now he thinks every man is Hannibal the Cannibal."

"You've been very rude," she said to Guy as she hurried him back upstairs. "I want you to promise that you'll stay here and be good. Otherwise, no funfair."

7

Guy didn't exactly promise but Laura had to leave him anyway, and gradually it began to dawn on him that he'd played this wrong. If he'd been nice, remembered his manners, he might have been allowed to watch the DVD in the sitting room. Keep his eyes peeled.

Men tried to smother women all the time. Guy knew this because he'd seen it on television. And he knew it was a bad thing because whenever it happened his grandma leapt up and switched it off. "Don't want to be watching that sort of thing," she'd say. At this very moment, his mummy could be getting smothered herself. He got up and went downstairs.

Laura and the man were facing each other across the candlelit dining table. Guy thought his mother looked an anxious shade of pink. "I'm sorry," he said. "Sorry I was rude."

"Why, sweetheart!" Laura got up and scooped him into her arms. "You good little boy." It added immeasurably to her pleasure in the evening to think that her son wasn't going to spend it upstairs feeling hurt and alienated. And looking round for his fire engine.

Over her shoulder, Guy studied the elaborate pudding. "Can I have some of that?" he asked. "With you?"

"Well, that would be lovely, wouldn't it?" said Laura, eager to reward this refreshing new attitude.

She sat Guy on a chair between Paul and herself and gave him pudding and an adult dessert spoon. Guy ate slowly and carefully, and as he ate he listened to the conversation. Not so much the words, a lot of which he didn't understand, but the tone. And it came to him that this was talk of a sinister nature. It was talk that played hide-and-seek round candles and flowers and wine bottles, and led, not by dint of what was said but by dint of what wasn't, to smotherings of determined and frequently naked proportions. Particularly on those TV channels that his grandma wouldn't let him watch.

He wondered that his mother allowed herself to be so obviously and hopelessly duped like this. It was impossible to see what attraction the man held for her. He made noises at his food that were never commented upon, went in for a lot of heavy-duty eye contact that he wasn't told was rude, and smoked so much that his insides had to be as black as a chimney sweep's brush. You only had to look at what smoke did to curtains, Grandma said.

"Would you like to hear about the newts in the school pond?" he asked in a tone that was as adult and compelling as he could make it.

"Why, yes," said Laura, delighted. "We'd love to, wouldn't we, Paul?"

"Of course," said Paul, but he didn't put much into it. By the time Laura brought coffee he'd had about as much of amphibia as he was prepared to take. His eyes met Guy's through a haze of cigarette smoke. They spoke volumes: *I'm on to you.* He left early and didn't offer to help with the clearing up.

*****

Being pleasant and conversational, Guy gradually learnt, was a more effective way of usurping his mother's dates than hitting them over the head with fire engines. Successful as that had been, he had an inkling that it was a ploy that couldn't have run for long. And now it turned out that all he had to do was be overtly sociable with these men - tell them about his day, maybe try to perch on their knees - and demonstrations of affection towards his mother and incipient smotherings became less and less likely.

Even telephone conversations - the ones where his mother gave her little laughs and played with her hair - could have their impact seriously lessened. He'd just nudge his mother's elbow and smile hopefully and she would say: "Oh, listen, someone here wants to talk to you. Here, sweetie, tell Joe how well you did at school today ..."

And Joe, exhausted after a day at the office, panting for a brandy, longing to hear Laura say, "Oh, darling, you sound so tired. Why don't you come round? Let me cook you a meal then press my lily-white breasts into your face ..." would be regaled with the life history of the frog and the doings of Rutherford, who apparently went into the girls' toilets at regular intervals for sundry purposes.

"Isn't he sweet?" Laura would say, taking the phone back about twenty minutes later and ruffling Guy's hair.

"Who? Rutherford?" Joe sounding much weaker now. Ready to settle for just a brandy at home.

"No, silly. Guy. He just loves talking to you. But I've got to dash, got to drive him to Cub Scouts."

*****

Once he'd got the hang of telephone numbers, Guy singled out certain individuals for special phone calls. And some man, maybe not as alarmed by Guy's attentiveness as he ought to have been in the past, but feeling pretty rough at being woken at the crack of dawn, would be jolted into life with tales of how it was possible to push a straw up a toad's bottom and blow down it until the toad burst.

"If he's going to ring me up," complained the recipient of the 6:30 a.m. exploding toad story, "can't he at least say something pleasant?"

"And you were never a small boy, of course," said Laura. "You never had a morbid fascination with things unpleasant."

"Well, I don't remember," said the complainant, uncertainly. "I don't think so."

"So that's why you're making up for it now, I suppose," snapped Laura, her voice heavy with innuendo.

Just occasionally, Guy would wish that his exploding toad stories could be treated with a degree of seriousness. Some man could say, for instance, "It's really not possible. I know because I tried it before I grew into a wiser and better person as a result of a big one across the bottom from someone who was prepared to straighten me out". It wouldn't be much but it would be something.

"Why don't these men want to talk to me?" he asked his grandma.

"They don't really want to talk to your mother," she replied, darkly.

"But they do," said Guy. "Talk to her."

"They're duplicitous," said Grandma.

Generally speaking, Laura's men lasted for about three months apiece, and their disappearances were sometimes sudden and sometimes protracted, depending on how hard Guy had tried to charm them. Laura had now passed her thirtieth birthday and she'd accumulated a lot of knowledge about computers, which stood her in good stead now that the life insurance was starting to run out, but nothing about men that stood her in any stead at all as regards replacing Guy's father.

"What's wrong?" she asked her mother, bewildered and occasionally tearful.

"Maybe they just don't like being liked," said Grandma.

*****

Until David John. David John had been raised in a big family, the youngest of six children, a little boy with a big capacity for love; to give it and receive it. You might have thought that five brothers and sisters would have given him all the opportunities he needed for both but, in truth, the reverse was the case. The John household was a paradigm for evolution - the survival of the fittest - and Mrs John was like a weary female bird with a big crowd of nestlings. She fed the one that opened its mouth the widest and squawked the loudest. David had to make do with what was left.

When he grew up and got round to girls, he tried to lavish all his pent-up affections on them. Not physically (which probably wouldn't have frightened them at all) but mentally, which scared them away in a very short space of time. Too needy, they said. Desperate. Sad. David's capacity for love was so great that it had to be spread around a bit - diluted so that people got just the amount they could handle.

The Johns were regular chapel-goers and eventually David ended up in the ministry. God was happy to be loved just as much as you felt like. Also, He had a lot of children, many of them crying out. They didn't always come to chapel, of course, the ones crying the loudest, so David didn't restrict his affections or his help to those who were prepared to sit through his sermons, short as he kept them. He helped wherever and whenever he could, and his love became a large and general and less intense thing altogether.

Until he saw Guy's mother. Dropping off old clothes for the latest crisis appeal in the village hall. David thought she was the most beautiful woman he'd ever seen and suddenly God, the members of his congregation, asylum seekers, several prisoners in nearby Broadmoor, a lot of youngsters at the drug rehab centre and the two old ladies he had tea with every Thursday, weren't enough. David felt a painful resurgence of his youthful need to love singularly and strongly. To get down on his knees for someone other than the Lord (who was big on offering opportunities to love but restrained on the response side of things). To have this beautiful woman simply put her hand in his and smile at him, for him, just *him* - that, David felt, would be the pleasure of Heaven.

Silently he stood and watched her, swallowing hard,

gulping down intensity. A big man with a big heart full of need but fluent only in words that catered to other people's needs.

But an enormous capacity for love wasn't David's only characteristic. Surviving five brothers and sisters takes tenacity, and David had some of that too. Eventually, he found out who Laura was and where she lived and, after a further long and anxious appreciation of the word "eventually", he asked her out to dinner.

"But, Laura dear," said Grandma, "he's a minister, for God's sake."

"Aptly put, Mother," said Laura, holding up dresses one after another.

"You know what I mean. Not a vicar, not Church of England, not a proper religion."

"He's a Christian, Mother," said Laura. "I've never appended myself officially to the business but I believe it's proper enough."

"You know what was going on in St. Paul's," said Grandma, shifting ground slightly. "All sorts of unnatural practices. Homosexuals gathering for tea and buns and God knows what."

"I'm sure He did," said Laura. "And I must remind you that the accepted view is that He doesn't mind. And neither do we."

"You're not taking my point, dear."

"I am, Mother. I'm just trying not to let it spoil my date."

"Guy won't like him like he's liked most of the others."

"Well, maybe he'll like Guy," said Laura wearily. "And maybe that's the most important thing."

*****

David listened to murderers and their lawyers, prostitutes and their pimps, addicts and their dealers, so listening to an eight-year-old boy out-talk him at the dinner table and prattle down the telephone about everything from the endlessly exploding toad to Rutherford's ongoing progress in the girls' lavs was pretty small beer. Besides which, he had learned from an early age never to expect exclusivity. To share Laura with Guy was no strain. He was not about to compete with a child for his mother, and he had love enough for both of them.

So Guy had a problem. And he knew he had a problem. He'd got past the age when he was under the developmental pressure of the Oedipus complex and reached a more stubborn one where he simply didn't like his mother servicing anyone's needs and emotions but his own. And now he was faced with a man who was big enough - both literally and metaphorically - to take anything that was thrown at him. A man who couldn't be charmed away by getting on his knee or driven away by monstrous behaviour. A man who knew all about turning the other cheek.

When David played football with Guy and his friends and Guy hacked him on the shins as often as he could, David simply bought a pair of shin pads to wear surreptitiously the next time - not because he couldn't stand the pain or minded having resentment worked out on his legs, but because he didn't want Laura to be embarrassed by the bruises.

In the manse after the Mother's Day service, when Guy deliberately dropped his orange juice full of half-chewed cake on the carpet, David was the first on his knees to mop it up. When he showed Guy a wren's nest in the garden and Guy picked out an egg, so tiny it was a miracle, and squashed it between his finger and thumb, David said, "Miracles are fragile things, Guy, and they don't come along every day. Especially if you treat them like that." He knew he trod a fine line when it came to remonstrating. He couldn't act too much like a father figure until Guy was prepared to accept him as one.

And until Guy was ready, Laura wouldn't be ready.

*****

"Well, I'll give him this," said Grandma. "He's lasted longer than any of the others. It could be that he's just stupider, of course. He must see that Guy doesn't like him."

"Or alternatively, he could be in love with me," suggested Laura.

"People who believe everything in the Bible can't be that bright," went on Grandma, as if she hadn't heard. "I doubt it's a more accurate piece of reporting than you find in the *Sun*."

"I think David appreciates its metaphors," said Laura.

"So you think he's in love with you, then?"

"Don't you?"

"It's a job to tell with these overly pious people."

"You know he's not like that," said Laura, wearily. "He's just a good man."

"God botherers bother me," Grandma sniffed. "They're desperately trying to sublimate something."

Laura, in turn, ignored this.

"Have you slept with him yet or is he a sanctity of marriage man?" asked Grandma.

"What?"

"You heard."

"I don't think it's any of your business."

"I just don't want you to marry him and then find out he's ... well ... got peculiar tastes."

"He hasn't."

"You're sure?"

"Yes."

"So you *have* slept with him?"

"We've been going out for six months and we're both in our thirties so what do you think?"

"I think you should look more excited about it."

"Guy gets upset if I look too excited. In fact he doesn't know it's going on at all, which means that there isn't any actual *sleeping* involved."

"So what are Methodist ministers like in bed?"

"*Mother!*"

"Well?"

Laura thought of the diffidence, the delicacy - and the earth-moving intensity that came with unselfish, unadulterated love.

"Divine," she said.

*****

Yes, Guy had a problem. And it wasn't the least of it that he occasionally felt a surge of real liking for this man. But, as yet, it was only occasionally, and the arrival of Christmas put an effective moratorium on surges.

"I don't know why we have to have Christmas totally rearranged to suit him," said Grandma, "him" being a piece of distancing terminology that she liked to apply to David.

"Because it's his job," pointed out Laura, for the umpteenth time. "And I want to support him. And Guy's over the Santa thing now, thanks to Rutherford, so he won't mind opening his presents later on."

"He will," said Grandma.

"I will," said Guy. Plus, he'd just had another belief straightened out courtesy of Rutherford. Smothering. An in-depth Rutherfordian interpretation of smothering, complete with anatomical drawings and sound effects. Now every time Guy saw David near his mother he felt sick. And highly disinclined to postpone Christmas presents to accommodate his chapel services. Or go to the fair with him.

Yet, equally, he recognised an inevitability about this man and, in the face of it, missing out on the Christmas fair could be a pointless deprivation. His mother had a hair appointment and David, on his own, wouldn't keep saying, "Now you're getting overexcited and you'll be sick. Let's just stick to hoop-la."

In fact they were at the hoop-la when Rutherford

turned up. A Rutherford who, whilst watching David's embroilment in goldfish snaring, broke out into nudges and winks and gory speculation about the exact nature of David's sexual relationship with Guy's mother. With his acceptance of this relationship teetering painfully on a knife-edge, Guy felt himself suddenly tipped into a physical revulsion that was gut-wrenching. Punching Rutherford in the stomach, he bolted. Running out of the crowds, he plunged into a side street and, flinging himself against a wall, sobbed into the brickwork.

He hated Rutherford. He hated David for doing things to his mother and he hated his mother for wanting to have these revolting things done to her.

A man en route to a parked car paused next to him. "You OK, son?"

Guy sobbed louder.

"You lost or something?"

Guy raised his face. The wolf man didn't recognise him after a gap of three years but Guy remembered him perfectly. "Get away from me!" he yelled.

"Hey, hey." Mike Chalmers raised his hands and backed away. "Only trying to help."

Guy's sobbing shot up a pitch. Mike Chalmers hurried away to his car, pursued by frightening childish invective. It was at this point that a panting David arrived. Rushing up to the sobbing, yelling Guy, he picked him up and hugged him hard. Catching sight of Mike Chalmers getting swiftly into his car, he asked, "What's happened, Guy? Who's that man?"

"I don't know." Guy had never known the wolf man's name. "He's a beast."

"What did he do?"

"He … he …" Wailing and struggling to be put down, Guy choked out barely intelligible words.

David hung on to him in horror. "He did *what* to your bottom? What did you say?"

But Guy only sobbed harder and kicked out at him.

"Christ," thought David, feeling sick with dread as he watched Mike Chalmers' car shoot away. "Oh, Christ."

*****

"I don't *know* exactly what happened," repeated David in anguish. "I was just trying to …" Foolishly, he held up a goldfish in a plastic bag.

"You'd better go," said Laura.

"Laura, *please*," begged David, tears filling his eyes, "I wouldn't for the world have let anything happen to him. And it was no time at all. Nothing could really …"

"I understand," said Laura. "But please leave. He'll be better with just me."

Guy was lying on the sofa, face bleached, eyes now dry but expressionless. Laura tried again to coax the full story from him. Guy ignored her.

"He's in shock," said Grandma. "Get him something hot and sweet."

To give herself time to get her own feelings under control, Laura went.

"Now listen to me, Guy," said Grandma in her hushed

voice. "David likes you, doesn't he? He hugs you and wants you to sit on his knee."

Guy stared stubbornly at the ceiling.

"There are men," went on Gran very slowly, "who like little boys too much."

Guy flickered for a moment. He was on a steep learning curve.

"These men have to be stopped," said Grandma. "Caught and put away for good."

Guy shot her a lightning glance. "Put away?"

"Where they can't hurt anyone."

"For good?"

"Yes," said Grandma. "Now, Guy. This man. The one in the alley who touched your bottom. Was it actually David?"

Guy gave the ceiling a long, thoughtful perusal. "Yes," he said finally. "It was David."

NO SEX AT SIMMONS,
SIMMONS AND SIMMONS

The brass plate on the office door read: Ms Virginia Mayden, Human Resources Manager. Inside, Ms Mayden was managing one of the resources who had been demonstrating an undesirable type of resourcefulness.

"Would you like to sit down, Mr Jackson?"

"Yes, Miss. Thank you, Miss."

"Don't call me miss, Mr Jackson. You're not at school now."

Mr Jackson, lowering himself into a tubular steel chair, rather wished he were. He'd known his ground there. For a start, nobody had styled themselves Ms, which he wasn't entirely sure how to pronounce, and he'd always been referred to as "Jackson", or alternatively, "that bastard Jackson". In either case, he'd always had a fair idea of what was coming next.

"Mr Jackson." Ms Mayden put her slim, manicured hands tidily together on her desk. "I'm afraid that yesterday afternoon, I received a complaint about your behaviour."

Jackson relaxed slightly. He was used to interviews that started like this.

"It was from Miss Byrd in Accounts – you know her, of course?"

Jackson nodded.

"Well, Miss Byrd was offended by some remarks that you apparently made concerning her blouse. Would you be good enough to give me your version of those remarks?"

Jackson thought about it. It seemed an odd request but he complied willingly enough. "I said it suited her."

"Anything else?"

"I might have said it was a nice colour."

"I see. And would you like to tell me why you said these things?"

Jackson shrugged. He'd just said them, that's all.

"*You just said them, that's all.*" Ms Mayden raised an eyebrow - not obviously plucked but, nevertheless, a delicately feathered arch. "Is that going to be your entire explanation of the matter? Your entire view of the incident?"

Jackson nodded.

"Mr Jackson," said Ms Mayden in a voice rendered exquisite by deep, concerned patience. "Why do you suppose Miss Byrd chose to wear that blouse this morning?"

Jackson had no idea.

Ms Mayden was pretty sure, based upon her own pattern of blouse selection, that it had been: a) because it was clean and ironed; b) because it was serviceable and appropriate; *and most definitely not* c) because it would draw the attention of male employees. And she explained this, thoroughly and carefully.

"Do you understand this, Mr Jackson?"

Jackson didn't, not really. No.

"I'm getting, Mr Jackson, at the fact that here at Simmons, Simmons and Simmons, we do not tolerate anything that could be construed as, or escalate into, sexual harassment. We keep sex *out of the workplace*. We treat all of our employees and our colleagues the same. Have you complimented Mr Smith on his choice of shirt today? No? Well then, you don't compliment Miss Byrd on hers. You understand the point of this policy, Mr Jackson?"

Jackson didn't say he thought it was ridiculous because he had, in fact, noticed Mr Smith's tie, and something of this opinion must have shown on his face because Ms Mayden felt obliged to elaborate.

"Let me put it another way then, Mr Jackson. Let us for one moment imagine – though it has to be said that, given your performance to date, this requires quite a leap of the imagination – nevertheless, let us imagine for the moment that you rise through this firm to become one of the managing directors. And let us further imagine that you have been given a very pretty and smart executive assistant. Then one day, you compliment her on her blouse. Now, you might have done this with the purest of intentions. Just to cheer her up. Or let her know that you appreciate how she always looks so perfectly the part. Or, it may have been simply because you've just signed a lucrative contract and are feeling particularly buoyant. The assistant, of course, doesn't know why you said it. And, consequently, she may misinterpret your motives. She may think that you are preparing to take a more personal interest in her. Maybe ask for a date, or even try to instigate something less polite. Not wanting any sexual involvement with you, either because she thinks it's inappropriate or because she sees you as nothing other than her boss, the assistant finds herself in a quandary. She's been made to feel uncomfortable but she doesn't want to offend you, so she thinks the best way to deal with the situation is to keep a little more out of your way. Naturally, this creates a problem. You, in turn and over the course of time, begin to misinterpret this new state of affairs. You suspect that because your executive assistant is less visible, she is less industrious. She is dodging work, dodging responsibility, and the eventual and unhappy upshot of this, Mr Jackson, is that the assistant is either demoted or loses her job entirely. And all because you chose to pass remarks about her blouse."

Silence. Possibly productive, possibly not.

"Mr Jackson?"

"Yes, miss?"

"Do you see the point of our policy, now?"

Mostly Jackson was wondering where, exactly, in the century of sex on the third, if not the first, date you could find a girl who was so helpless that she would be unable to handle a compliment about her blouse without losing her job. Obviously, up in Accounts in the person of Miss Byrd. Though she wasn't exactly a girl. You could look at a chicken a long time before you thought of Miss Byrd.

"Mr Jackson?"

"Yes, miss?"

Ms Mayden finally smiled. "I've made a memo on this, Mr Jackson, but it isn't a first warning. This has just been a chat to explain to you how we do things here. I want to be certain that you understand our policy perfectly, together with the reasoning behind it."

"Yes, miss. Thank you, miss."

Coming out of the office, Jackson bumped into Mr Smith whose shirt he had signally failed to comment upon.

"Yo, young Jacko," said Mr Smith. "Been having your resourcefulness managed in an unharassed and sexually democratic fashion?"

"Miss Byrd," said Jackson gloomily, "thinks I've been coming on to her."

"And have you?"

"She's got to be forty, if she's a day."

"But a real FOB," Mr Smith pointed out.

"True," agreed Jackson who, though vague on "Ms", understood FOB perfectly.

"Nevertheless," said Mr Smith. "This is the age of the new man, and you youngsters with your unfocused testosterone must learn to disengage your balls from your mouth or go and get jobs on building sites." He paused for a thoughtful moment before resuming his progress along the corridor. "Though the building site as a bastion of bum cracks and wolf whistles is under siege even as we speak. A source of fleeting regret to some perhaps, *le dernier cri* of toxic masculinity."

Jackson looked vaguely after him, wondering what a *dernier cri* was. And what Mr Smith *really* thought about it. This was all so much harder than school.

Ms Mayden, meanwhile, was thinking that she deserved a cup of coffee. She felt that the interview with young Mr Jackson had gone well. Hopefully, she'd guided him without dispiriting or emasculating him. Because Ms Mayden wasn't a radical feminist—a member of SCUM (The Society for Cutting Up Men) or FOFUCC (Female Order For the Use of Chemical Castration). She just wanted to fulfil her brief to turn Simmons, Simmons and Simmons into a flagship for equal opportunity employment, emphasising a clamp-down on sexual harassment.

In her desk drawer, neatly typed, she had the pertinent points of the Equality Act of 2010 which stated that sexual harassment can be any unwanted sexual behaviour that violates another's dignity, makes them feel intimidated, degraded or humiliated, or creates a hostile or offensive environment. She'd made a list including the following: jokes made on the basis of sex; a colleague discussing details of their sex life; unwanted sexual attention outside of the office, e.g., office parties or after-work drinks; unwanted sexual advances on social media. These she'd transferred onto a flyer (to be handed out where appropriate) along with details of the website "Rights of Women" and the telephone number of their legal advice line. She was, she thought, fully in command of the situation and prepared for all eventualities. She swung her legs out from behind her desk with a contented smile.

Ms Mayden's legs were not emphasised in any way by her knee-length skirt or her flat pumps, but they were exceptional legs. More exceptional, for instance, than Miss Byrd's—a fact that had not escaped Jackson even though his eyes had never visibly drifted in their direction.

Ms Mayden could have had coffee brought to her office but she preferred to walk to the machine on Level 4—both to stretch her splendid legs and to take the opportunity to have a few words with Tanya, who was PA to the youngest Mr Simmons. Tanya and Ms Mayden were not natural soul mates, but their respective jobs threw them into orbits slightly outside those of most of the workforce, and so they tended to come together. Tanya was not as beautiful as Ms Mayden but she was younger and more enhanced. Her hair was three shades blonder, her makeup was more dramatic, her breasts were more elevated and pressed together and her skirts were tighter and shorter. And she could do all of this, Ms Mayden reflected contentedly, in the full knowledge that she was not giving any of the male workforce the wrong idea, because it was beginning to be understood at Simmons, Simmons and Simmons that women dressed to please themselves and not to stimulate men. A woman who wanted her nipples outlined by her blouse did not want them stared at, or commented upon or, heaven forbid, brushed against, but was merely expressing control over her own sexuality. In short, she was empowering herself.

"So," said Tanya, whose relative isolation as a PA did

not, somehow, isolate her from gossip. "How did you get on with Jacko?"

"Mr Jackson took the point, I believe," replied Ms. Mayden. "He's young. He'll learn."

"Learn?"

Ms Mayden raised one of her elegant eyebrows and said: "Learn to keep his sexual inclinations and preferences out of the workplace. And maybe - just maybe - handle them with a sense of responsibility and thoughtfulness when he's elsewhere."

"Can't fit Jacko and thoughtfulness into the same category, somehow," said Tanya, delivering a hefty thump to the coffee machine. "Plus, it seems to me that work is exactly the place to find somebody with those common goals and interests that are touted as necessary for a lasting relationship."

"On the contrary," said Ms Mayden spiritedly, "work is not the place to strike up personal relationships because the power and proximity problem skews one's judgement. The causes and effects of an engineered hierarchy, and the dominance of the senior employees over those more junior, complicates the correct procedure for judging people on the basis of who they are, as opposed to what they are."

"So the point you are trying to make," said Tanya beadily, over the rim of her plastic cup, "is that just because the youngest Mr Simmons - the fabulously rich and handsome Mr Simmons - is my boss, it doesn't mean that he has a big one or is in any way superior in his knowledge of how to use it effectively."

"Thank you, Tanya," said Ms Mayden. "Once again, you have managed to reduce a complex argument to its most basic and primitive …" She stopped. She was unable to finish the sentence, or even the thought, because walking towards them was, well, if it wasn't Henry Cavill it was his clone. Her face flushed, her legs felt suddenly wobbly and she had the strangest feeling in the pit of her stomach.

"What was that about basic and primitive?" asked Tanya.

Though at the office Ms Mayden industriously levelled the playing field upon which the workforce surged to and fro, actively reinforcing the viewpoint that colleagues and teammates were neither male nor female but simply colleagues and teammates, this did not mean that she was impervious to the differences between men and women. In her minimalist flat, watching *The Man from U.N.C.L.E.* for the third time she was specifically aware of the fact that she would, given a sufficiently effective seduction period, be prepared to get into it with Henry Cavill but not with any of the other men. Nor any of the women.

But not once in her three years at Simmons, Simmons and Simmons had she felt, let alone shown, a sexual predilection for any of the men there. So, it was with some alarm that she now found her eyes starting from her head.

"That," said Tanya with a smile, "is Professor Braden Swain."

Guiltily aware of a gut reaction that was far from convenient, Ms Mayden said, "*Who?*" And in a transparent attempt at a cover-up, asked, "Where?"

Though Tanya was capable of overlooking large bundles of mail, together with equally large sections of Mr Simmon's appointment book, she missed nothing when it came to male/female interaction. At this point, Professor Swain conveniently turned off into an office.

Tanya smiled. "He's seriously something, isn't he?" she remarked.

Ms Mayden knew that it would be ridiculous to try and fool Tanya over anything that didn't pertain to the purely intellectual, so she settled for displaying a level of natural curiosity. "But who is he, exactly? And why is he here?"

"He's doing research into sexual harassment."

Ms Mayden's mind went alarmingly blank. She had a degree in sociology, plus a desk drawer and a new computer each replete with every type of decree that pertained even vaguely to political correctness, but she suddenly felt as *au fait* with the more subtle levels of sexual harassment as a pole dancer. Had she expressed this, Tanya would have no doubt suggested to her that a pole dancer would be quite capable of handling sexual harassment in any of its more usual manifestations without the patronising benefits of a flyer, a website or a helpline.

"*Research?*"

"Professor Swain has a degree and a PhD in anthropology, more letters after his name than you can fit on an envelope and a chair at an American university. At the moment, he's investigating the British situation re sexual harassment. Specifically in the workplace." Tanya might have been sketchy in certain areas of her job but she certainly knew how to find out what she wanted to know.

"How we do it?" asked Ms Mayden, a shade weakly. "Or what we do about it?"

"Bit of both, I suppose," said Tanya who also knew, and generously revealed, that the American anthropologist was thirty-five years old, single, possessed of appealingly tight buttocks and muscular thighs, jogged every morning after breakfast and drank only water. But her anthropological interest pretty well tailed off after that. What Professor Swain was actually going to put into his research notes interested her little. "I'm sure he'll be coming to talk to you." She smiled broadly.

It was at this point that Ms Mayden began to regret her flat pumps. The American was a tall man and, though she was elegantly ballerina-like, she was starting to feel oddly stumpy. She also regretted her blouse. These were all new sensations to experience as a result of a visit to the coffee machine and she preferred not to scrutinise them too deeply because they amply demonstrated, she told herself rather hotly as she climbed the stairs back to Level 6, why it was so important to keep anything to do with sex right out of the workplace. She'd left Tanya a little hurriedly in order to think over the Henry Cavill /anthropologist conflation in the privacy of her own office. She wished that one of the Simmons brothers had had the courtesy to warn her about the visit. Or that Tanya had had the wits, or the generosity, to bring up the subject the day before. Someone turning up to do research in what was essentially her specialism and her cabbage patch could pose an intellectual challenge that she didn't want to fluff. This, she told herself repeatedly, was the real reason that her heart was beating more rapidly than the heart of a slim twenty-eight-year-old, who has just climbed two relatively short flights of stairs, had any right to do.

When her heart rate and breathing had settled back into their respective resting rhythms, she sent an email to the offices of the brothers Simmons requesting that she be informed whether or not Professor Swain's schedule would include a visit to her office or a requirement for her cooperation. She received a reply to the effect that it was apparently difficult for an anthropologist to have a schedule because anthropologists were in the business of observing and noting behaviour, which had to be done when behaviour was there to be observed and noted. This made for an unpredictable diary. It was possible, of course, that Professor Swain would be interested in her personal viewpoint - although it could in no way be allowed to affect the purity of the primary scientific process which was, as previously stated, one of observation.

Ms Mayden looked at this for a long time, wondered who on earth had written it, messed with the subtext a bit and came up with absolutely nothing that would guarantee that she could, within the vulnerable hours before five o'clock, do anything about her blouse or her flat pumps or, more significantly, enhance her level of expertise in this new and suddenly expanded universe of sexual behaviour.

She kept out of the staff dining room at lunchtime. (A dining room where there were no tables set aside for the hierarchy and no mechanism by which those whose schedules were dictated by phone calls to New York or Hong Kong or the handling of millions could get any faster service than the person who emptied the paper shredders. It didn't matter, of course, because they didn't eat there.)

Ms Mayden ate a packet of sugar-free Polos reflected upon the fact that the following day was the firm's Christmas party. In fact, she thought, Professor Swain had come at just the right time to get a really big slant on sexual harassment. She wondered if this could be viewed as weighting the scientific process but then he could, for all she knew, have a section specifically labelled: "Office Parties UK, Behaviour At".

On the other hand, it would be a pleasure to attend a party where there was a man who drank only water and didn't, therefore, lose all concept of personal space. She would be able to talk to him sensibly, enhancing her appreciation of her own job. And she would drink nothing but water herself, thus ensuring that she would be in full control should another of those inconveniently spontaneous gut reactions make itself manifest. (The blame for which she was shifting, progressively and even convincingly, onto the shoulders of excess caffeine.)

*****

By the time the office party began at 6:00 p.m. the next day, Ms Mayden was in complete control of herself. She was wearing a very smart, black, fine wool suit with a beautifully cut jacket and a ... well ... shorter than usual skirt.

Underneath, she wore a rich red, silk camisole top with spaghetti straps – which would *not* keep sliding off her shoulders because she would never remove the jacket. The ensemble went rather well with her shoulder-length blonde hair but, and this was the important part, it was an outfit that she could well have worn on a normal day. Ms Mayden wasn't for taking clothes to work and changing as if it were a school party.

At 5:55 p.m. precisely, she'd combed her hair, added a bit of mascara and a smidgen of lipstick of a much paler shade than the camisole. Shoe changing at work she found acceptable - after all, some people walked there in trainers - so it was with a clear conscience that she took off the flat pumps and replaced them with a pair of patent leather sling-backs with four-inch heels.

She'd intended to be at the party punctually because she was in some sense hosting, but she was waylaid outside the lift by a marginally pregnant employee who didn't think that the light levels in the building were sufficient to stimulate correct foetal development. Ms Mayden was familiar with the principle but not the wattage, and such are the conversations that can be floated on the subject of pineal glands and fluorescent light that the party was in full swing before she got to it.

In spite of her faith in the policies of Simmons, Simmons and Simmons, and the deep respect and appreciation in which she was certain most of the employees held them, she somehow had a feeling that those same employees must now be providing a traitorous amount of fodder for Professor Swain.

"Well, he's here," said Tanya, surveying Ms Mayden from mascara and lipstick via camisole to shoes.

"Who?"

Tanya didn't even acknowledge that. "Over there with his notepad and his bottled water. So very much the new man. Testosterone free and non-invasive. You're going to love him."

The party was taking place in the dining hall, tables and chairs relegated to the edges. There was a buffet of the cold chicken drumstick and sausage roll variety, gluhwein, punch, and paper decorations. None of it was quite as salubrious as Simmons Bros could have run to. The rather intrusive Christmas party album had made it as far as Wizzard's "I wish it could be Christmas every day ..." Ms Mayden sighed. Had nobody written anything new?

She worked her way round the outside of the crowd, pausing now and then to speak to this one and that one, until she finally came to Professor Swain, who was standing at one end of an empty table, alone except for his Perrier water and his clipboard. She drifted behind his right elbow and took a casual look at what he had found significant enough to commit to paper.

He had two columns. The one on the left was headed "Observation" and the one on the right headed "C and C", which Ms Mayden thought could mean compare and contrast, or check and confirm, or consider and conclude ... or ... Pointless speculation. She read quickly, catching as much as she could. The writing was not entirely legible but certain words were printed, especially in the C and C column.

The left-hand column began more or less as follows:

Aesthetic appreciation / lookism / verbal comments about clothing

Close dancing / conceptual rape

Mistletoe / osculatory rape

The right-hand column "C and C" was more expansive, including things like:

Handshakes: primarily a masculine ritual of recognition

? an affirmation that serves to exclude females

? Man shaking the hand of a woman borders on sexism

Check N.H. on Body Politics.

The professor was currently continuing his lists with, in the left-hand column:

Newspaper open at page 3.

Naked female torso.

And opposite, under C and C:

Glanced at by passing males;

ref. the Venus of Willendorf

Hostile environment harassment?

Check equal employment opportunity commission for civil rights status of this in UK.

Ms Mayden needed no more confirmation that she was in the presence of an expert. This expert presence, on the other hand, was signally failing to register *her*. Unless his peripheral vision had been disrupted by his hugely attractive Clark Kent reading glasses, she was cutting no visual ice with Professor Swain at all. Nevertheless, she felt that it was her duty as the firm's HR manager to make herself known to him.

"Excuse me, Professor Swain," she said. "May I introduce myself? I'm Virginia Mayden, the human resources manager here."

"Ah, Miz Mayden." Professor Swain whipped off his glasses, thus revealing the most divine pair of soft brown eyes that were... well ... just the sort of eyes you would want looking at you when ... A graphic image erupted unbidden from Miss Mayden's subconscious - or somewhere - and fairly startled her, falling as it did within the category of conceptual rape. Strangely enough, once the initial shock had worn off, she didn't feel as guilty as she ought to have done. In fact, she was left with a pleasant tingly feeling which she presently put down to Christmas spirit and goodwill to all men.

"I'm pleased you spoke to me," went on the professor, running a hand through his thick, dark hair in a half-shy, boyish way that would certainly have enabled an accusation of conceptual rape to stand up in a court of law had the situation been reversed. "I didn't want to speak to you first because a man must not assume that he has the right to engage a woman in conversation any time he pleases."

"*Really?*" This was a new one on Ms Mayden. Or possibly a carefully selected chat-up line of impressive originality.

"Yes, really," said the professor. "It has been noted in a certain survival manual entitled *Back Off* that verbal attack is the most prevalent form of violence against women."

So, it wasn't a chat-up line. "Were you intending to attack me verbally?"

"Of course not. But one must never ignore the continuum theory. Anything that is uninvited initially is potentially assaultive and there is, indeed, an established link between casual conversation and progression to the ultimate violence of homicide or what we should, in fact, call gynocide."

"Gynocide?"

"The killing of women by men."

"Right," said Ms Mayden. "Well, Professor, the fields here must look ripe for the slaughter to you. I can well imagine how many uninvited conversations you've observed."

Professor Swain gave a laugh that showed off to perfection the brilliance of his white teeth.

"You've been pulling my leg, haven't you?" said Ms Mayden.

"I think not." The professor replaced his glasses. "That would most certainly come under the category of social touching which is, I believe, a level three sexual harassment which I would never dream of committing."

Was it just the fairy lights or were his eyes twinkling? Certainly, he was still smiling.

Ms Mayden shook her head. "You could be somewhat ahead of me in this business, Professor."

"Call me Buck," he said. "I'd prefer that, if you'd be comfortable with it."

"Totally. And you must call me Virginia."

"My home state. Couldn't be better."

They surveyed the scene before them in silence for a few moments, and then the professor said, "But you must excuse me. I'm supposed to be observing here, and eliciting comments from the observed at moments when I think they're likely to tell me the truth. And there might be more of this truth forthcoming if they didn't see me with you. However, I *would* like us to talk further. Would it be possible to meet outside of working hours? At a time and place of your choosing, naturally."

Ms Mayden wondered whether or not she could interpret this as a date, decided that that was a decision she was not yet in a position to make and suggested a civilised but not ridiculously expensive restaurant that lay within walking distance of the office. As Americans tended to eat dinner early, the agreement was that it would be appropriate for the pair of them to go straight there from work the following evening.

"Well?" Tanya caught up with Ms Mayden, who was now wandering round rather vaguely with everything slightly out of focus. (To celebrate her little success she'd had a couple of glasses of punch, about 80 proof, that tasted like paint stripper.) "Did you get him to speak to you?"

"I did."

"Did you learn a lot about sexual harassment?"

"An amazing amount. And more to come, I believe."

"But did you experience any?"

"Not nearly enough. But more to come, I believe." Ms Mayden gave a huge giggle.

Tanya looked hard at her. "Virginia? You okay?"

"Never better. And listen, I found something out in my

swift perusal of Buck's notes. Something that may well be to your advantage."

"Buck? *Buck*? I thought he was called Braden."

"Buck to his friends," said Ms Mayden. "Obviously. But listen, if you make a pass at the youngest Mr Simmons and he responds then it is actually him, not you, who is guilty of sexual harassment. I believe this is called receptive non-initiation."

"Right," said Tanya. "Useful. But if he doesn't respond? Which he hasn't so far."

"Well, if he gets sufficiently irritated, you'll be sent to me and I'll charge you with a civil rights violation and then I'll fire you."

"Virginia, are you sure you're all right?"

"You know, Tanya, that's one hell of a dress."

Tanya was wearing a black slinky thing that was mostly straps and lacings and probably had to be stapled onto her.

"And I feel very proud," Virginia continued, "that you can actually wear an outfit like that to an office party and have the youngest Mr Simmons treat you exactly as if you were wearing a bin liner. I think it says a lot about the success of our policies here. Don't you?"

*****

The following morning found Ms Mayden in a quandary. The paint stripper hadn't done her much good but the lingering nausea was nowhere near as irritating as the fact that she had worn her most fetching and well-cut suit for the party the evening before. So now, she couldn't think what else she had that would be able to progress seamlessly from work to a restaurant, to a potential date. Without the hypnotic, flashing fairy lights, the warming, six-foot-two proximity of Professor Swain and the potent punch, she was much less optimistic about the fact that this *could* be a date. On the other hand, if it wasn't, the outfit that she wore could well have an influence on whether or not it turned into one. This principle didn't apply within the walls of Simmons Bros, of course, but in the uncontrolled environment of Fernando's Brasserie with someone who was not, in truth, a fellow employee, Ms Mayden had a distinct feeling that the difference between a polo neck sweater and a low-cut dress could be very significant. It ought not to be, of course. Which raised a few ethical and moral considerations that became subsequently submerged amongst more pressing aspects of the putative date/business dinner. Such as:

a) Men were notorious for both noticing and not noticing what women wore. A cognitive variable that pivoted round many things, including the level of cover provided by the item of clothing and whether or not the man was married to the wearer.

b) The black suit that she had worn for the party had probably passed unobserved.

c) With a different coloured camisole top (emerald) it would look just as good today as it had yesterday.

From 6:00 p.m. Ms Mayden stood for forty-five minutes in the building's lobby. A period of time during which she studiously avoided any review of male/female stereotypes which could have led her to the inevitable conclusion that she was not the one who ought to have been kept waiting. Plus, as she had previously been informed, anthropologists had to observe, and they had to observe until the subject matter had the civility to fuck off elsewhere. Ms Mayden clapped a hand over her mouth and cast a furtive glance at reception in case, in her impatience, she'd actually said that aloud.

She couldn't believe some of the things she'd been thinking during the past forty-eight hours. Bad, unbidden things had been going on in her head and her stomach and some other places that she didn't want to draw attention to. And it had all begun with the advent of Professor Swain. He had dropped into her life like a meteor and there was no telling what size hole he was going to create.

His apologies when he arrived were profuse, obviously heartfelt and though largely unheard, proved remarkably effective. Though less effective than his broad shoulders, trim waistline and warm, firm handshake.

The handshake was a courtesy that was curiously in contrast to the notes he'd made concerning their political correctness. But Americans seemed to shake hands as a form of greeting, Ms Mayden had noticed, even with people they'd met the day before and the day before that. It was a cultural thing that was probably difficult to reconcile with its new anointment as an offensively exclusive form of masculine affirmation.

The restaurant was only a quarter of a mile away and, as it was a fine and relatively mild winter evening, they decided to walk and enjoy the Christmas lights. Sometimes Ms

Mayden was on the outside of the pavement getting the exhaust fumes and the splashes, and sometimes it was Professor Swain. It all depended on how they had dodged round the buskers and the dog walkers and the hot-chestnut braziers, and which shop window they'd each elected to look in.

The door into Fernando's Brasserie was heavy and had uncooperative hinges. (**We are open. Please push hard.**) So it was fortunate that Professor Swain with his wonderful shoulders arrived there first. It was less fortunate that the door's swift rebound swing, obeying some perverse law of mechanics that outwitted stiff hinges, caught Ms Mayden a big one on the nose. She staggered into the restaurant, fumbling for a handkerchief with her eyes watering. Her nose was one of those noses that bled easily. Some people can go a lifetime and never have a nosebleed but Ms Mayden was a martyr to them. She hastily excused herself, leaving Professor Swain to get the table, and hurried to the restroom where she dripped into a washbasin with her eyes raised in desperation to the mirror. *Why hadn't she put out a hand to hold back the damned door?*

After what looked like the expulsion of at least a pint of blood, the nose stopped dripping. Ms Mayden splashed her face, reapplied foundation from her bag, combed her hair and went back into the restaurant.

Fernando flapped around concernedly. He knew Ms Mayden but he did not know her new friend who spoke pleasantly enough, but somehow exuded the resonance of a very expensive American claims lawyer.

Ms Mayden had been hoping for an intimate table for two in the shadows - after all, there were enough of them - but Professor Swain had organised something one could barely reach across. And it was situated right under the main chandelier. Was he expecting more people?

"I'm so very sorry about your nose," he said. "I should have held the door but well ... Doors are complex things, aren't they?"

"Are they?" asked Ms Mayden who was, all things considered, feeling slightly miffed. "I thought they were relatively simple contrivances designed for the purpose of keeping things in and keeping things out."

"But they are a minefield when it comes to sexual etiquette," said Professor Swain, earnestly. "Male gallantry can so easily slip into patronage. According to Marilyn Frye the opening and holding of doors can be viewed as imitating the behaviour of servants to masters and, as such, becomes a form of mocking behaviour towards women who may then feel themselves deemed to be servants and caretakers of men in a phallocentric society. Door opening, even when accepted as chivalry, can send women a clear message that they cannot deal with the world without perpetual assistance. Moreover, the detachment of the door-opening act from the concrete reality of what women need and do not need is a message that women's needs and interests are unimportant or irrelevant. And please note that I am quoting a highly respected source."

Ms Mayden stifled the reactionary thought that this respected source had to be a hypersensitive idiot with a deft command of words but a serious lack of self-esteem. "Fine," she said. "Well, on the way out, I need you to hold the door open until my nose is through it. That's a statement of *my* needs and I'd be obliged if you'd remember it.

"Also," she went on, "due to the possible swelling of this aforementioned nose, I'd be further obliged for a little less illumination."

"I am highly attuned to women's needs," said Professor Swain with a slow smile that, rather annoyingly, swept away most of Ms. Mayden's lingering sulks.

He snapped his fingers. "Waiter?" Within seconds they were moved to a highly desirable and very intimate table where he was so close to Ms Mayden that she felt bathed in his body heat from head to toe.

"This okay?" he asked. "This invasion of personal space?"

Ms Mayden smiled.

"You have to say 'yes,'" he said. "Nil verbal has to be taken as a 'no.'"

"It's perfect," she said. "And so is the eye contact. But I'm not in the picture as regards tables."

"Tables for two," said Professor Swain, "suggest coupledom. Even reflect a male-dominated society's insistence upon it. To keep a woman under the control of an individual man is more efficient than keeping women in ghettos, camps or even sheds at the bottom of the garden. I quote here from the Leeds Revolutionary Feminist group of which you may be a member."

"I'm not." She'd never thought of Leeds as quite such an overtly activist place.

"Nevertheless, by moving to this table you have accepted the principle of coupledom. The principle of you and me as a prospective couple."

Ms Mayden smiled again.

"You have to say 'yes'," Professor Swain reminded her.

"Yes," said Ms Mayden with a bigger smile. She was getting this now. It was a courtship ritual conducted on terms that were within their joint field of interest. It was informative and amusing and (apart from the nose - which wouldn't have happened if the door had been lighter) remarkably compelling.

The waiter reappeared at this point to take their order - which, of course, they'd barely had time to consider.

"Now," suggested Professor Swain, "we could get into some erotic food play which the University of Maryland has placed on its official list of unacceptable and non-verbal behaviours that constitute sexual harassment."

"I must put up a notice in the works' cafeteria," said Ms Mayden. "Tanya says that being fed is sexually stimulating. I've never tried it myself."

When the food arrived Professor Swain offered her a forkful of his steak tartare. "Yes?"

"Yes." Ms Mayden closed her eyes as it went into her mouth.

"Working?" He offered her another forkful. "More?"

"Yes, please."

"Obviously, you're not a vegetarian."

"No."

"You realise of course that meat eating and male

dominance are overtly associated?"

"I hadn't," confessed Ms Mayden. "Tell me about it."

"According to Carol T. Adams," said Professor Swain, "the presence of meat proclaims the disempowering of women."

"So having you actively feed it to me means what, exactly?"

"It means, among other things, that were we in the US at one of the radical universities I'd be heading for the giant claims court. But, for the here and now it means ..." He leaned forward and whispered something in her ear.

"That was verbal rape," said Ms Mayden. "To say it is to do it."

"The very act of requesting permission to perform a sexual act may in itself constitute verbal rape," said Professor Swain. "It's a Catch-22 situation. Makes it hard to get anywhere."

"I really can't concur with that," said Ms Mayden, who had eaten all of his steak tartare and fed him all of her spiced shrimp. "Seems to me, you're managing very nicely."

"Tell me what you found out at the office party," she said, when the main course arrived.

"Apart from the fact that you were the most beautiful woman there?"

"You could tell me about that as well."

"Do you want to hear the one about flattery and sexual coercion?"

"No," said Ms Mayden. "I'll just take the flattery for

now and deal with the sexual coercion when it comes."

"Flattery can be defined as praise commonly given to women in substitution for money and occupational status."

"And conversely, would you like to hear some comments on the insecurities and small penis size of the men who withhold flattery because they think it may somehow undermine their power and dominance?"

"I would, actually." Professor Swain got out his notebook.

"You know," said Ms Mayden, over the pudding menu, "we can dictate how people behave but not how they think. Do you believe that at the personal level of the male/female interface we are changing things or merely burying them? Boys like Jackson, hormonal time bombs, are still under the influence of a strong biological imperative."

"It's how the imperative is played out," said Professor Swain. "That's what we change. These things must be done correctly. And with care. And I believe that repetition of correct action gradually moves the Overton window."

And he gave her another of those smiles and Ms Mayden had another of those tingly feelings which proceeded to overpower her need for any further discussion on the subject of Mr Overton and his window.

Fernando, still conscious of the weight of his restaurant door, supplied them with an exotic pudding on the house, which Professor Swain said was very kind but very dangerous – interpretable in a court of law as proof of acceptance of guilt.

It took some soothing on Virginia's part to calm Fernando after this - and to persuade him to leave the pudding which looked divine. All the more so when it started heading her way on the tip of Professor Swain's spoon. Buck had such nice fingers, she thought dreamily. Strong but sensitive-looking. Tanned but slightly ink-stained. A perfect combination of the animal and the academic. Fixation on small details was, she knew, a sure sign of infatuation. But she didn't mind. It just felt too good.

They split the bill and she didn't mind that either. She knew that splitting bills was the correct and emancipated procedure - though personally she'd have gone for a simple 50/50, not troubling with the minutiae of who had eaten what.

"I fly home in two days," said Professor Swain, piling up pound coins.

"To the US?" asked Virginia, fatuously. The remark had jolted her. She'd been having a disjointed but stimulating fantasy in which Buck, compelled by his intense attraction to her, had either acquired a chair at a British university or arranged an academic exchange. And between these vague negotiations in which he'd transferred his career from one continent to another, there'd been more detailed ones that involved beds, new silk lingerie and the Kama Sutra, which Virginia had never read but was nevertheless managing to visualise in glorious technicolour. So it was disconcerting now to have to try and telescope all of this into forty-eight hours – sixteen of which had to be ruled out on grounds of work with a further significant percentage reserved for sleep. Maybe.

"So …" went on Professor Swain, "that brings us to a chunk of conversation that's going to be difficult to conduct in a truly PC fashion." Having stopped scrutinising the bill he took off his glasses and put them in his top pocket.

Virginia looked at his wonderful eyelashes and said: "Then don't. I'll write you a waiver." And she picked up a napkin and wrote: "I give Professor Braden Swain carte blanche to say whatever is in his mind without fear of accusation, recrimination or litigation."

"You'll have to sign it," said Professor Swain, reading upside down with a widening smile. When Virginia had finished writing her name with a flourish he picked up the napkin and put it in his pocket. "Come back to my hotel with me."

"To examine your research?"

"To examine whatever you want to examine." He smiled. "We'll do exactly what you want. Step by careful step. Because I'm leaving, we can't have a long courtship but we can have a very thorough one."

Virginia chided herself for leaping to the unemancipated assumption that it would make her look like a slut to put out on the first date. Women's empowerment surely shouldn't include concepts like "slut". That was the double standard. Besides which, if she turned this down she'd never get to sleep with Henry Cavill. And even if she *was* behaving like a slut, Buck wouldn't be around as a constant reminder and she would certainly enjoy her next viewing of *The Man from U.N.C.L.E.*

"I'll come," she said.

"I'll see to it," said Professor Swain.

*****

He apparently had a pretty good expense account. Virginia glanced around as they entered the lift in the local Hilton. She didn't see English research grants running to this. The room was a classy concoction of coffee and cream lifted by bright Impressionist prints and a bowl of fruit. It was immaculately tidy except for a pile of papers and a couple of textbooks stacked on a writing table in front of the window. Somebody had already drawn the curtains and put mints on the pillows. The bed was king-size.

"The bathroom is here," said Professor Swain, opening a door, "if there's anything you want to do in there."

"I'm curious about how big my nose has got," said Virginia lightly, thinking that she was really supposed to be having a vaginal douche, inserting a diaphragm, fidgeting through some Feminex and making a selection from assorted condoms. She had none of these things with her. In fact, she had none of these things. Since her life had become dominated by a career in which she was busy insisting that there should be no sex at Simmons, Simmons and Simmons, she'd had no sex.

She looked around the bright space and studied her face in the dazzling mirrors and decided that her nose wasn't as bad as it could have been. Then she opened the bathroom door and said, "I wasn't expecting this. I don't have, you know, the necessary equipment or anything."

Professor Swain opened a bedside drawer and held up a couple of foil packets.

"Fine," said Virginia, going back into the bathroom. She would have felt more special if the condoms hadn't been quite so handy. A quick dash to an all-night chemist might have been more gratifying but, she reasoned, empowered women ought not to be disturbed by premeditation. She splashed around a bit - using some of the hotel toiletries while she empowered herself - and then she went back into the bedroom and gave Buck a brilliant smile. He didn't notice because he was studying a black leather-bound book the size of a Filofax but not a Filofax.

"That your little black book?" she asked carelessly.

"It is."

"Is it full?" She worked up another smile.

"Half-full."

Half-full was pretty full, really. Addresses and telephone numbers were brief things. And you'd imagine that compulsory PC negotiating techniques would have trimmed the field a bit. A lot of red-blooded women might walk away from a man who banged restaurant doors on their noses, selected King Arthur-sized tables and was nervous of eating meat in case it emphasised anything that could smack of toxic masculinity.

"That's a lot of women, Buck," she said, nodding towards the book. He really didn't seem ... well ... that sort of man.

"Only five or so."

How could five women take up so much space? Did they come with complete CVs, financial statements and the results of recent physicals? And why was he looking at them now?

"This book," said Professor Swain, running his fingers over the smart binding, "was put together by Angela H. Schlinkey, a hotshot Californian lawyer."

"Was she pimping for you?" asked Virginia. "Or was she just responsible for developing this fine line in leather-bound stationery?"

Buck gave her a very odd look and Virginia gave him another brilliant smile and decided that they were obviously talking at cross purposes. "So does she feature in there?" she asked. "This Angela H. Schlinkey?"

"I assure you," said Professor Swain, putting the book down and taking off his jacket, "that she has one of her own."

"Right." Virginia's interest in the book was being supplanted by an urge for a brandy. Buck, she noticed, had continued to drink only mineral water throughout the meal and she, mindful of how giddy the party punch had made her and not wanting to look like a lush, had followed suit. But now her gaze kept wandering uncontrollably in the direction of the minibar. This man was divine to look at – could turn out to be divine in all sorts of ways (though certainly unusual in some) - but right now, in this most intimate of situations, he wasn't putting her at her ease. A man with a book full of women really ought to have developed a little more … smarm.

Obviously noticing the suction the minibar was giving off, he suddenly said, "I think it's best to do this stone-cold sober."

"Most people don't," said Virginia, crossing to the bed. "Most people getting into bed with virtual strangers like the wheels oiled."

"But then they aren't in command of the situation," said Buck, wagging the hotel ballpoint at her. "Things become emotionally cloudy, consent becomes confused. Expensive lawsuits follow. No, I think that a couple having sex should be aware of every little detail. It should all be done very slowly and carefully. And savoured, of course. Lookism coming up," he added, giving her a very appreciative appraisal from head to toe.

Well this is more like it, Virginia thought. Now we start. She took off her jacket and Buck hung his on the back of a handy chair. Then he picked up the book again and, opening it wide and bending back the spine, laid it in the middle of the bed with the hotel ballpoint placed to keep a specific page.

Virginia sat gently on the bed so as not to disrupt it and looked questioningly across at him. Buck met her eyes, his own suddenly soft and encouraging, his lips parted … Her eyes flew helplessly to his mouth.

"Feet off the floor?" he asked.

Slipping off her shoes, Virginia swung her legs up onto the bed and lay back on the pillows. Buck bent over her and his smile warmed her like a fire. "Comfortable?"

"Yes."

He laid his considerable length beside her, the mattress dipping slightly so that she naturally rolled towards him. "Okay?" he whispered.

"Yes."

It was a ripe and perfect moment. He pressed the ballpoint pen into her hand. "Tick here then, and sign your name."

"What?"

"Shhh …" He lifted her hair off her neck and ran his fingers appreciatively through its silkiness. "We're just playing it by the book."

She felt the softness of his lips on her neck - a feeling enhanced by the slight roughness of his evening stubble. An irresistible undertow caught her. She scribbled helplessly in the vague area of the indicated line.

His mouth wandered softly over her face. "Kiss?"

"Yes, please."

"Sign here."

She scribbled again. And what a kiss. A minute-long miracle of mingled tenderness and frank desire.

"Should we take the camisole off?" he whispered, unbuttoning his shirt. Virginia looked at his smooth, tanned pectoral muscles. Felt the irresistible warmth of his body reaching out to her.

"Why not?" she breathed.

"It has to be a 'yes.'" The book appeared in front of her face. Focusing her eyes with difficulty she read: "I the undersigned do hereby agree to the removal …"

She stopped reading. "Am I," she asked slowly, "going to have to sign this book the second before I come?"

"Well, certainly the second before *I* come," said Buck.

"You know," Virginia sat up and pushed him away, "let's just not."

"Not come? Okay … well … One rather assumes that that's rather the point of the process but I know that a lot of women have already ditched penetrative sex – all orifices – because it smacks of invasion and domination and it may well be that the loss of control a woman feels during orgasm could be a threat to her …"

"STOP!" Virginia shouted.

"Excellent," said Buck, "a very clear 'stop'. Women have to make it obvious when they mean 'stop.' A lot of court cases have been lost because …"

"Stop *talking*." She stood up. "Now, listen to me. I'm a fully grown and currently sober woman, and I know when I want to be seduced. And I'm perfectly capable of negotiating the details of that seduction nicely and subtly as we go along."

"Well, that's exactly what we're doing," said Buck, slightly surprised. "Negotiating." He held up the book.

"Without Angela H. Schlinkey in the mix," said Virginia, dangerously.

"But this is just making it legal. Ensuring there is no accidental coercion. Safeguarding your rights as a woman."

"I don't want to be safeguarded," hissed Virginia, suddenly furious. "I want to be transported. It's my right as a woman to be transported and that's never going to happen if I have to keep *stopping* to fill in sequential contracts with the bloody transportation mechanism." And she headed for the door, fighting her way into her jacket, juggling her handbag and pulling up the straps of her slingbacks.

"How about a tape recorder?" Buck shouted after her as she wrenched the door open and stormed out into the corridor. "We could cooperate nicely over mike placement and sound levels ..."

"Kiss my ass," Virginia shouted back. "Have you got a page for that?"

*****

Eight thirty in the morning, a couple of days after the "date", and Ms Mayden, sitting in her office at Simmons, Simmons and Simmons, was still fuming. Not so much at Professor Swain personally, though there was certainly scope for that, but at the fickleness of Fate in sending her a Henry Cavill clone, a fantasy male specimen, who could only mate by numbers. It was ridiculous, she thought over and over again. Political correctness taken to the point of idiocy. And she felt even more annoyed that she had overcome her natural reservations about sex on the first date to indulge in such a punctilious and ludicrous charade.

It was just an unfortunate coincidence that this was the moment that Miss Byrd from Accounts chose to arrive, requesting an interview re the continuing behaviour of Mr Jackson. She wanted it seriously noted this time, she said, that Mr Jackson was persisting with his comments on her clothing. She wanted him to receive an official warning, indelibly engraved in black and white on his personal record.

Ms Mayden studied Miss Byrd judiciously. "That is, in fact," she said finally, "a very nice top that you're wearing."

The top was not the point, explained Miss Byrd. She felt that that which was undergoing scrutiny was not, in fact, the top but the contents of the top. In other words, her breasts.

"I see," said Ms Mayden. "And was Mr. Jackson abusive about your breasts? Did he criticise them in any way at all? Did he threaten them?"

"Of course not," said Miss Byrd.

"Did he touch them? Did he, heaven forbid, stand on them? Could we have him for trespass?"

"Certainly not," said Miss Byrd. "I wasn't lying on the floor."

"So he merely, you think, admired them? Inwardly?"

"I should say so, yes."

"Would you be so good as to tell me your vital statistics, Miss Byrd?" Ms Mayden poised a pen over some paper in an officious fashion.

"38, 26, 38."

"Thank you. And would you be so kind as to raise your skirt and have a good look at your legs? I'll turn my back if it will make you feel more comfortable."

"Not necessary," said Miss Byrd, hoisting up her skirt.

"And your conclusion? Have you come to an honest opinion about your legs, Miss Byrd?"

"I would say that they were pretty good legs," Miss Byrd admitted. "For my age." She was obviously puzzled and slightly irritated, but clearly confident that this had to be the official way forward. Ms. Mayden had never been noted for frivolity.

"Thank you, Miss Byrd. Now, would you tell me, to the best of your knowledge, how old Mr Jackson is."

Miss Byrd shrugged. "I don't know, exactly," she said. "I suppose he must be nearing nineteen by now."

"Exactly," said Ms Mayden. "And do you know the predominant characteristic of the eighteen or nineteen-year-old male, Miss Byrd? No? Well let me tell you. He has more circulating testosterone in his body at that age than he will have at any other point in his life. Biologically speaking, he is at his sexual peak. In other words, he can get it up more frequently in a given space of time than he'll ever be able to manage again without pharmaceutical help. And the unfortunate developmental anomaly that accompanies this situation is the fact that, in common with that of every other human being, his prefrontal cortex, the rational part of his brain, isn't fully in charge until he's about twenty-five years old. This makes it difficult to keep the arousal system under control during a period when there is so much circulating fuel."

Silence.

"So, Miss Byrd, it's not surprising that Mr Jackson is currently noticing your breasts, is it? Breasts being, as they are, prominent secondary sexual characteristics."

Miss Byrd was indignant. "Just because he notices

them," she replied, pinkly, "it doesn't mean that he has to comment."

"I thought the comments were about your top?"

"Well yes, but the breasts are inside the top, aren't they? One has to assume that they are, in fact, what is being observed."

"Given the amount of toxic masculinity that is supposedly swilling around in the world today, one would certainly be predisposed to think so," said Ms Mayden. "So let me commend you on the fact that you keep your breasts quite assiduously within the confines of your tops. They are certainly sizeable breasts, and we wouldn't want them attracting any more attention than they already do. But, however many rules we bring in, it will continue to be difficult to prevent Mr Jackson's hormones from prompting him to notice them. We can call it lookism, we can call it inappropriate aesthetic appreciation, we can call it conceptual rape, we can call it mental groping, we can call it whatever the hell you like, but the fact remains that all of these are merely verbalisations of an imperative that is very difficult to police. Not least for Mr Jackson himself, with his prefrontal cortex lagging so inconveniently behind the curve. That does not mean, however, that we can't *try* to ensure that he learns to react appropriately for each and every situation in which he finds himself. Agreed?"

"Totally. And that's what we are doing, isn't it?"

"It is. In a manner of speaking. But you know what I *really* think, Miss Byrd? I think that in this particular situation, the best person to teach Mr Jackson what *is* and what is *not* appropriate behaviour in his contact with women is not an HR manager with a list of rules and a helpline backed by a selection of legal options, but the women with whom he comes into contact. We are screaming our empowerment and yet we are under the impression that we cannot cope with an eighteen-year-old boy, even in a safe environment, without the nanny state to back us up. I think that is a shameful state of affairs. Don't you?"

Miss Byrd was not an instant convert to this point of view. "But …"

Ms Mayden interrupted her. "The situation is, Miss Byrd, that you are a good twenty years older than Mr Jackson, and you *know* that you are a whole lot cleverer. Moreover, speaking frankly and without prejudice, I suspect that you are also a kilo or two heavier. So, my suggestion would be that you go out there and either a) take his comments in a spirit of superior and somewhat sardonic or patronising amusement or b) tell him, in whatever words you find most appropriate, just to fuck off!"

*****

It took only two hours for the brown envelope to arrive on Ms Mayden's desk. She knew what it was. In fact, she was already emptying her drawers. There was something she needed to do. Somewhere along the road to ultimate emancipation, feminism had taken a wrong turn. She wanted to set in motion something that would run against the extreme ideas of SCUM and FOFUCC. A countermovement with guidelines not yet perfectly elucidated but evolving carefully under the working title of: "Women in favour of better seduction." Acronym (to be reviewed because when read aloud it had a curious ring to it): WIF of BS.

THE IMPORTANCE OF BEING EDDIE

"Are you Eddie?"

Sam thought about it for a moment and then glanced over his shoulder. He wasn't Eddie but then neither was the guy behind him because there wasn't one.

"I'm so pleased," she said. "Pleased that we decided to do this."

Sam put an empty glass on the bar. Do what? "Thing is, I'm not ..."

"No," she said, a little breathless now. "Neither am I. But that doesn't matter, does it? We don't have to rush into anything, do we?"

That sounded fair enough to Sam. A lot fairer than having all the pretty girls walk past him to greet other guys. Not that many pretty girls came into the back bar of The George hotel at eleven o'clock in the morning - which made this one look all the more stunning. Honey-coloured hair, honey coloured skin, she looked like she'd taste of honey all over. Sam's imagery, but he'd have been the first to admit that he wasn't an expert on tasting girls. The ones that he looked like he had a chance with were - well, honestly speaking - the sort that if they asked you if you wanted a taste you'd think, now let's see, how hungry am I? Is she all that's lying between me and starvation? Supposing I was on death row, the condemned man being offered a last breakfast? Now would I, if she was what was on offer? Her or just a long walk to the electric chair with my stomach rumbling? Sam thought he'd go to an empty death. Plus he worked in the hotel's kitchen, a place where you didn't get much of a yen for food.

Everyone, especially his parents, said he could do better. Than the kitchen. People had been saying that about him since he'd been slow to sit up. A year old and still flat on his back so that his toys, including those bought for the purpose of developing intelligence and manual dexterity, had to be dangled over his face on pieces of string. A laconic baby. Hard to motivate. All the signs of growing into a person who couldn't be motivated at all unless he was hit between the eyes with something. Must do better. He's really going to have to shape up soon if he's going to make something of his life. An A level in art isn't going to get him far. Employers want people who can work computers and spell. If all he can do is draw he should have been a caveman or a Renaissance Italian. Even cartoons have to have captions that use actual words. But Sam came with no caption. No writing underneath to explain him.

By the time he left school with his B grade in art his dad was beginning to think they'd brought the wrong baby out of the hospital. A mistake that seemed all too easy to make in the heat of the moment: "Yesterday in court, a white couple with a black baby and a black couple with a white baby accused St. Mary's maternity unit of being lax with labelling procedures."

Sam's dad had sired a child who could do physics and advanced maths and work investment portfolios, yet now he had one who washed plates and peeled vegetables and came home and picked up a sketch pad and drew women with wings (not angels) and monsters coming out of rock crevices. He'd once sneaked away some of these drawings and shown them to the psychologist at work. The psychologist had looked at them from all angles and pronounced them to be inner demons.

"Christ!" Sam's dad had been exasperated. "How many inner demons can a twenty-year-old who's been brought up in a white, middle-class household where the parents don't row or get drunk or abuse him, possibly have?"

"There's a naked woman here," said the psychologist, "with three breasts and a tail."

"Shit! Let me look at that."

"He's beyond me," he said to his wife in despair when he got home.

"But they like him up at that hotel," she replied. "He might be a disappointment to you but he's keeping *them* in immaculately scraped carrots."

At this precise moment, however, the carrot scraping was nor receiving its due attention.

"I'm Alice," said the girl. "But of course you know that."

"Of course," said Sam, who thought he could explain

about not being Eddie when they got to know each other better.

"Should we have something to drink here?" she asked, looking round. "Coffee,maybe?"

"Why not?" agreed Sam.

"Because Eddie's going to be turning up any moment now?" suggested the barman, as Alice set off for a table.

"Or maybe not," said Sam. "And besides, she obviously doesn't know what he looks like. And vice versa, with average luck."

"So you don't think he'll be alerted by the fact that she's the only girl in here?"

"Not if she's with me." Sam followed Alice to the discreet table she'd selected.

Dark was fine by him. He'd started work at six-thirty that morning without a wash or a shave. Dark was good. But what was better, what had stunned him, was that this girl, so much the sort of girl he'd always wanted to know - beautiful, classy dresser (Sam couldn't put a price tag on clothes but he knew cheap and these weren't) - could not only accept that he was Eddie, but seem in no way disappointed with the fact. Sam knew disappointed like he knew cheap, and she wasn't either.

Of course, this thing they weren't going to rush into needn't be what he was assuming it was. Maybe she'd come with the intention of buying a car from Eddie, renting a room above his shop, giving him clarinet lessons.

"So tell me all about the Amazon," she said.

The Amazon? Eddie was an Inca or something? This

was going to be a lot harder than clarinet lessons.

"Long," he said. "And those piranhas got a bigger rep than they deserve."

"And the Bilhazia?" She smiled.

"Bill who?"

The telephone behind the bar rang. "It's for you, Eddie," said the barman.

Sam went across, leaning casually on the counter, drifting subtly towards a corner.

"What do you think you're doing?" the chef shouted in his ear. "You're supposed to be in the storeroom. We need more parsnips here. *Now!*"

"I'm there," said Sam. But even Chef, madder than hell, couldn't make him as preoccupied with where he should be, as with where Eddie was. And should be. Still…

"Look," he began as he sat down next to Alice again. So far she hadn't taken her eyes off him. Whoever this Eddie was, she was certainly keen. And not because he had a car for sale. "I've done the stupidest thing …" And he really meant to follow this up with a confession about his non-Eddieness, but she turned to look at him with such anxious blue eyes, her neck curving so beautifully, a slim golden column above perfect collarbones that, well, maybe it was the artist in him, or maybe it was the fact that Eddie, the ingrate, was making this incredible girl wait when he, Sam, would have died first - he just couldn't say what he ought to have said.

"I've forgotten an appointment," he blurted. "An important one. Not," he rushed on, "as important as you.

But maybe less easy to reschedule."

It took him about five seconds to realise that reschedulable wasn't going down, and a lot longer to gloss it over with much repetition of more successful words like thoughtless, abject and devastated. Sam might not have been great at spelling apologies but he was rapidly learning how to string them together effectively. But he still had to leave.

"I'll call as soon as I'm free," he said, turning over a beer mat and offering it to her.

"I'm having a bad day," he went on, "what with all this overbooking, so let me not mess up the telephone number as well."

After some hesitation and a bit of lip pursing she wrote it down.

"Email?"

"How on earth could you forget that?"

"I forget where the dots come. Humour me."

She wrote: alipiranha@xmail.com.

Of course. How could he forget that? She got up and walked away then, slightly confused and obviously hurt.

"Here, Sam." The barman pushed a kitchen overall across the bar. "Good job you'd just spilt tomato juice down that."

"I wish I'd dared ask for her address."

"It's Eddie you need to know about," said the barman. "Like who he is, for instance. He might be a humourless son-of-a-bitch."

"You've never heard of an Eddie?"

"No."

"You're sure? I mean, he picked your bar as a meeting place and it's hardly Lovers' Central. Can't you think of anyone he could be?"

"No-one," said the barman. "But if Eddie comes in here regularly, believe me, she doesn't want to get too excited about him."

"On the other hand," he called, as Sam set off for the parsnips, "she looked pretty excited about you. Could be she's easy pleased."

On his way to the kitchen, Sam passed the hall porter and enquired after Eddie. An Eddie in his twenties somewhere and without a surname. The hall porter and Eddie were unacquainted. Sam also quizzed the receptionist about a regular guest, who maybe travelled with stops at The George. An Eddie. Even an E. No luck.

In the kitchen, he scraped vegetables and asked everyone who passed through - which was a lot of everyones, The George's kitchen being the epicentre of all manner of things - if he or she knew an Eddie.

"Who the fuck's this Eddie that Sam's getting so worked up about?" asked the chef, exasperated. "Is he some sort of gay?"

Wincing, Sam went quiet for about ten minutes after that. Then he caught sight of the head waiter who had once worked at the Negresco in Nice and was reckoned a bit of a world traveller. "Do you know anything about South America?" he asked.

"I know it's got killer bees and snakes that swallow you

whole and football teams that ditto. Why?"

"I was wondering if Eddie could actually be South American."

"If I saw you on the streets of Bogota you'd be the one I'd ask the way to the British Embassy. He can't be. But this reminds me of a bit of information that *is* a cert. You're off the hotel's five-a-side because you run like a girl."

Sam didn't regret the football but all these heartless un-PC comments about faggots and girliness were starting to disturb him. He took a couple of passes by the kitchen mirror. It was for the waitresses to check that their hair wasn't getting too wild for silver service and the steamy bloom on it helped their complexions a lot.

Sam's stubbled chin somehow looked more designer and less got-up-too-late than it had felt to him earlier. The jawline had undesirable tendencies, true, but girliness wasn't one of them. And the Adam's apple, that was a man thing, wasn't it? And his nose wasn't what most women would have wanted, though not necessarily a disaster for him - not pug or retrousse or generally undesirable like Gerard Depardieu's. Deep-set White Hunter eyes for scanning the glittering expanse of the Amazon. Nothing puppy dog there.

So it had to be the hair. He had hair that put a man in a zone where he had to work hard to pull it off. It grew in disordered tangles that could have served very well in a seventies metal band but which were almost impossible to coerce into anything that accorded with current fashion. He'd shaved it all off once, shaved it half off twice, paid out fitful fortunes for smart barbers and each and every time he'd felt in accord with nothing – not even himself. If his hair had been ginger instead of a mousey brown it might have worked perfectly alongside a big red nose and a pair of exploding trousers. Plus, it was a constant source of irritation to the chef: "Wear the fucking hairnet thing, will you? We don't want bloody Byronic locks near the food." The head chef was another part of Sam's life that refused to conform to prevailing norms.

Yet the girl hadn't really seemed to register what he looked like. And this, Sam felt, meant that he was in deep trouble. Deeper than he would have been with Gerard Depardieu's nose. Bearing in mind his own earlier and rather churlish reflections, he knew that not caring what somebody looked like usually came along later. It wasn't how love sprang up between people at opposite ends of a bar. It was how it finally struggled forth between two old friends, who weighed 120 kilos apiece, had really bad hair and lacked initiative. Underneath each 120 kilos, bad hair and lack of initiative there was, of course, a gleaming jewel, glimpsed only briefly at times, like the flash of sun on glass, but finally so endlessly dazzling as to outshine hundreds of kilos worth of physical challenges. And when two by 120 kilos were fully dazzled they fell in love. Yet Alice and Eddie hadn't even met. There had to be something so spectacular about Eddie at a distance that his looks had already been rendered totally irrelevant. But what the hell was it?

"His voice," said Kath, one of the waitresses. "I could

fall in love with a voice. Over the phone, you know. Sean Connery's voice, for instance."

"And if you didn't have a mental picture of Sean Connery - and a forty-year-old one, I hope?" asked Sam. "If, when you saw this man, he looked more like Danny DeVito?"

"But you don't look like Danny DeVito, do you?" And Kath disappeared with a loaded plate in each outstretched hand and one balanced on each upturned wrist.

Sam didn't think it could be Eddie's voice. If he'd been doing a Sean Connery or a James Earl Jones down the phone, Laura would have known her mistake the minute he, Sam, had opened his mouth. Eddie had to be a man of undistinguished accents. Either that or they'd never talked on the telephone. Maybe the Amazon was a dead spot.

"So he writes," said Kath, coming back for another load. "Fantastic love letters. Emails. He's poetic. Like him with the big nose in *Roxanne*. The Cyrano de whatsisname business."

"Yeah, yeah, yeah," said Sam, who had more or less seen this one coming. "You know what? Poetic men brass me off. It's just a literary form of sexual harassment. A get-her-into-bed routine that favours intellectuals. I don't like it."

"Nor me," said the chef. "Only pussies write poetry."

"I'd like a song," said another waitress. "Someone who wrote a song for me and sent it on a disc with red ribbon and some roses."

"Bummer," said Sam. "You could shut me in this

kitchen until I turned to stone and I'd never come up with a song."

"Or money," said the chief washer-up and pan-scrubber. "I could fall in love with a man who looked like hell and could write sod all but a pound sign followed by a one and several zeros. He wouldn't even have to marry me. And I'd wash his dishes too."

"Sam," said the window cleaner, who had come in for a cup of tea, "you know what it is about Eddie? It's what he does. His job. That's what you need to find out. What Eddie really does. You are what you do. Now me, I'm a window cleaner. It catches no girls, believe me. Forget those 'Confessions of a Window Cleaner' movies from your grandfather's time. At least six times a day, I knock on a door and a woman's voice calls, 'Oh Christ, it's the window cleaner again.' And a man's voice calls back, 'Can't he just do the upstairs? Honestly, he's a bloody rip-off. A ladder and a fluffy mop and it's like a licence to print money.' And then in the evenings, at the pub, you know, or the disco, I'm doin' okay and then she asks, 'What do you do?' Two minutes later she's back with her friends."

"Well the only thing I know about Eddie is that he's been up the Amazon," said Sam.

"'Nuff said." The window cleaner drained his mug and stood up. "If this bloke is fuckin' Tarzan you might as well forget the girl now. Scraping carrots isn't going to do it for her."

"But you aren't what you do," Sam protested.

"Trust me." The window cleaner shook his head.

"Don't get into it. Scraping carrots is like having six toes. You do better to keep your socks on."

"But you aren't what you do," repeated Sam. "Are you?"

"How can you not be?" said the window cleaner.

"And how can you pretend to be Eddie when you don't know anything about him?" asked Kath.

"It's a tough one," agreed Sam, "but I'm working on it."

He looked at his orange fingers. Was he entirely a man who scraped carrots? Couldn't he have layers?

Nevertheless, the truth of the matter seemed to be that a guy who couldn't write poetry or songs or cheques that ran into double figures, obviously had three strikes against him in the charisma department right away and if, on top of that, he scraped carrots for a living then, clearly, he might as well kiss charisma good-bye.

But then he thought of Alice's silky lashes and wonderful, smooth shoulders. He took the beer mat out of his pocket and looked at the hastily scribbled telephone number. As soon as he'd finished work he was going to call her. After all, she'd seen him and hadn't recoiled. In his books that put him ahead of the game. Of course, he had to get the phone call right. Think of the perfect words to say. He wasn't a poet, true, but how hard could it be?

"Hey dreamy boy," Chef yelled at him. "I'd like those parsnips *today*."

Sam finished work at four o'clock and called Alice three times, when she was respectively washing her hair, drying her hair, and too far down the garden to be brought back.

This information was supplied by her mother who, if she knew about Eddie, had no obvious intentions of helping him out. So that could be viewed as encouraging. Possibly.

The fourth time Sam rang, he stepped out into the high street because the rest of the staff were starting to giggle. This time he got Alice herself who thanked him in a soft, breathy voice for the lovely explanatory e-mail - which he hadn't sent, of course, but which entirely renewed his dislike of poetic men. Still, it had got her in the mood to agree to dinner at The George at eight thirty that evening, though she was obviously surprised that he could get to Reykjavik and back in the course of a day. *Reykjavik*? Eddie couldn't do one damned thing in Brighton or somewhere?

*****

Sam ran back into The George, found Kath the waitress and gasped, "Favour. *Please.*"

"Is this about that Eddie again?"

"About Eddie's girlfriend. She's agreed to have dinner with me here at about eight thirty. Ask Chef if he'll do me all the works and let me pay for it at the end of the month."

Kath looked undecided.

"Oh, go on. I've been irritating him all day and he fancies you."

That was true and Kath knew it. Sam followed her to the kitchen and hid behind the door as she walked across to Chef and prattled in his ear while he frowned and cocked his head, whisking furiously at a sauce and trying to follow her gist. Even Sam was barely able to get it. Jeez, he thought, no wonder she feels the need to get it on with a poet.

"Sam wants to have dinner with his gay friend?" Chef asked finally, waving his dripping whisk in confusion. "On deferred payment terms?"

"Not with his gay friend. With his gay friend's girlfriend."

"*What?*"

"No. Look, the friend isn't a gay. And he isn't even a friend, come to that."

"So why does Sam want to have dinner with him, again?"

"Not with *him*. With the girl Sam's trying to steal from him."

"Well that's more like it," said Chef, his face clearing. "Tell Sam dinner's on me. Would he like the special?"

*****

On his way home Sam called to see Chas Reynolds - an old classmate and science nerd who had grown into a hobbyist hacker. One of those guys that GCHQ should track and recruit before the Pentagon applies for an extradition order. With uni out for the summer Chas was jacked in, in his parents' basement, studying cosmology and one or two other things that made Sam lose a clear grasp of certain aspects of human anatomy.

"I need some information about a bloke called Eddie," he said, finally. "Could you hack into e-mails that have gone to alipiranha@xmail? She must have saved them."

"Who's *she?*"

"A girl to die for."

"And Eddie? Is he some sort of gangster, then?"

"I didn't mean literally die." But yes, Sam thought, Fast Eddie. That ran off the tongue. So what sort of name *was* Eddie? If he'd been called Torquil Tremaine or something, you'd get a picture. You'd also know, quite certainly, that you were never going to be in it. A man called Torquil Tremaine had to live up to more than you could ever compete with.

"He's not a gangster, then," said Chas, after fifteen minutes of key clicking.

"No." Sam peered over his shoulder. "Much worse. He's a real hunk of hero sandwich, isn't he? A world saver. A man who scours jungles for cancer cures. All muscular concern and a bit untamed round the edges. Greystoke with a bloody degree. I'd rather he'd been Torquil Tremaine."

"Who?"

"Oh, nobody."

"Don't get all worked up," said Chas. "Originally, she met him in a chat room on fucking flowers. How untamed can he possibly be?"

"And look," he flicked up another e-mail. "These aren't great photographs. Mostly of groups with a few brown people in there. All the white ones have beards and are desperately in need of some soap. Worst news is, he says he's this one who looks about six foot two. Unless the rest of them are really small." He glanced at Sam. "I'd never noticed *you'd* got that tall. All that hunching over sketchpads should've given you a Quasimodo hump. But look, he doesn't exactly write up a storm of sexual promise. Nothing to get her really juiced. Oh no! Just a minute. What's this? No shorts and streams of urine?"

"Stop," said Sam, reaching for the off button.

"Hey." Chas grabbed his wrist. "You need to read this stuff 'cause you're never going to think of it for yourself. Look … swims up the urine stream into your urethra. That's in your dick, you know. Oh, shit, it's a parasite in the river. Gets you if you pee."

"Bilhazia," said Sam in relief. "I wondered who he was."

"I reckon you could market it to local councils," said Chas. "For swimming pools."

*****

Sam sat down to dinner in his father's double-breasted suit, which was a lot too big around the waist (which he thought she wouldn't get to find out) but perfect across the shoulders (which was, after all, what stuck above the table). He'd called at the unisex hair salon and he was now as near Hollywood hero material as it was possible to get for thirty pounds. Plus he had the advantage of being a lot taller, Hollywood selection procedures mysteriously favouring men who had to wear stacked heels in order to kiss what he assumed were average-sized women. But the thought uppermost in Sam's mind was that it was going to be hard to be a botanist. Latin hadn't been his strong suit at school, along with a lot of other things. So he wanted to keep clear of botany. And plant hunting in general, plus large tracts of

South America and the whole of Reykjavik, at the same time as promoting conversation about things which she would find deep and meaningful but which wouldn't necessarily mark out a college education as different from the one you got in the kitchen at The George.

"I want to talk about you," he said.

"What do you want to know?"

"Well, let's start at the beginning. Were you born here, in this town?"_

"Yes. Well, no, not specifically. Mum had to go to a bigger hospital. I was a yellow baby. Jaundice, you know. Comes of blood groups not matching well, I believe."

"So straight away we have something in common," said Sam. "Bad babies."

"You were yellow?" `

"I was slow. A baby who could never pass his neurological assessment tests. A baby who was beaten repeatedly on the knees and the soles of his feet with little wooden mallets, while the doctors said things like, 'This baby doesn't react to his environment. If we don't fix him he'll be heaved off the survival ladder by everybody pushing past him.'"

"Well, obviously they fixed you," said Alice.

"No." Sam raised his glass and looked reflectively at the wine. "I don't think they ever did. Maybe that's how come I ended up in the Amazon. It's less crowded there."

"But not the place for someone who doesn't react to his environment."

"I'm learning," said Sam. "I'm also talking and it's supposed to be you."

So Alice talked and Sam listened. Not that he heard much, though he knew exactly how her mouth curved when she said certain words, and how her eyes lit up when they were words that really fired her, and eventually how her hand felt as he held it across the table. When the headwaiter asked how the food was, "sir," he had no idea.

"You only have a couple of days, don't you?" said Alice.

Sam came out of his state of lovestruck hypnosis with a jerk. *I do? Before what?*

"And so ..." she went on, "I ... well normally I'd never suggest this ..." (She was already a fetching pink colour so Sam thought, *I believe you; please go on.*) "... but, well, it seems as if we've known each other a long time and well ... maybe you wouldn't like to be the one to suggest it but maybe ..."

"Yes?"

"Maybe we could get a room here."

Sam was speechless. The hand that held hers went into reflex spasm. The George wasn't fully booked. He could wangle a room for nothing, but that wasn't the point. Using another man's identity to have dinner with the girl of your dreams was one thing, but going to bed with her on the back of a CV you didn't have was quite another. Somehow, during the fantasies he'd been having all day, he'd imagined that he'd have time - time during which Eddie failed to materialise and he, Sam, the real Sam, took his place.

"Oh, God," said Alice, now well beyond pink, "I've said the wrong thing, haven't I? You think I'm ... You don't want me."

Sam seized her other hand and squeezed it fiercely. "I do want you," he said. "I want you more than I've ever wanted anything in my life. It's just that … well, there's something I must tell you."

He searched desperately for suitable words - though how suitable he could actually make "I'm not Eddie" at this stage of the proceedings was giving him some trouble - when over the top of her beautiful, bewildered head he caught sight of the barman gesticulating wildly at him. Important hand signals, mouth working silently. *Come here. Now.*

Sam excused himself, relieved at the reprieve, and went out of the dining room into the corridor.

"It's Eddie," said the barman. "He's in the bar."

"The real Eddie?" asked Sam, suddenly faint - a feeling that had been waiting to make itself manifest ever since the word "room" had come up.

"How many fake Eddies can there be, for chrissakes? *Yes*, the real Eddie. And he's looking for her." The barmen jerked his head towards the dining room.

"How did he know?"

"Beats me, but I think you'd do better to skip out through the kitchens. Now."

"He looks in the mood for a fight?"

"Actually he looks mostly inscrutable. But inscrutable as if he's trying really hard to suppress something big. Which, you being up here with his bird, he probably is." Pause for thought. "Actually he looks like somebody on TV or in the movies who can turn into something else if he isn't very careful."

"The Hulk? Bruce Bannon?"

"No. Different sort of somebody else who's got something really big to suppress. My daughter keeps watching them all the time. That's the trouble with girls, you know, they just won't watch *X-Men* or *Ironman*." The barman's brow furrowed for a moment. "*Twilight.* That's it. Those *Twilight* movies. That vampire, you know the one."

"He looks like Edward?" Sam felt faint again.

"Sort of."

"But he's a botanist, for God's sake. He's meant to look like … I don't know. Somebody off a gardening programme."

"What can I say?" The barman shrugged. "They're just not screening botanists like they used to."

Sam pushed his hair back and looked sadly into the dining room. "It doesn't matter," he said, dully. "I was just about to tell her the truth, anyway. I suppose I was holding out a minuscule hope that she would say, "Oh Eddie's nothing to me now I've eaten coeur à la crème with raspberry coulis across a table from you. But of course I was fooling myself. And now he's down in the bar looking like every female's fantasy. Well, at least I haven't blown it totally for her. Keep him there till she comes, will you? Give me time to explain. To apologise."

"I'll do my best," said the barman, "but if he turns into a vampire in the meantime, I'm not pushing it."

Sam went back to the table but he didn't sit down. Alice was looking anxious. Hurt. Anxious again. And beautiful.

"Look," said Sam. "There's no easy way to say this so

I'll just say it. I'm not Eddie."

"*What?*"

"When you came into the bar this morning I wasn't Eddie and I'm still not Eddie. But you were … are … so lovely that I lied. I couldn't help myself."

It was easy to hurt Alice if you were Eddie, Sam could see, but if you weren't Eddie - well, she held up better than he'd expected. She took the napkin off her knee, crumpled it fiercely and slammed it on the table. "So who are you?"

"I'm Sam Jenkins."

"And who is Sam Jenkins?"

"I work here. In the kitchens."

"You cook?" She glanced for a moment at the remains of the coeur à la crème and Sam saw a small window of opportunity through which he could have slipped as a chef and maybe earned himself a small compliment. Duped by a prospective participant in the *Great Cook-Off*. Maybe not so bad. He cooks you dinner, you know, and ah, well …

"I scrape the carrots and stuff," he said.

Her eyes rolled and hit the ceiling. Sam accepted it. The window cleaner was right. Some things are fundamental; beautiful, accomplished girls don't go for men who work as skivvies in hotel kitchens. Or, if they do, the kitchen is Spanish and they are on holiday and when they get back home it makes them feel bad. They have to take a holiday-after pill to get over it, and the following year they go somewhere in a boat with Greenpeace people and watch whales.

She looked at him. "Well," she said. "I suppose you

finally passed the neurological tests. You learned to react to circumstances." She paused for a moment and tears sprang suddenly into her eyes. "So where's Eddie?"

Sam handed her his father's clean and beautifully ironed, spotted handkerchief.

"No need to cry," he said. "Eddie is in the bar where he should have been this morning. And when you see him, I don't think you'll have too much trouble forgetting me."

And he turned away and walked slowly across the dining room. People watched, but only casually. The bill for dinner at The George could come to seventy pounds a head without wine. For that you got a clientele that was so self-involved it noticed little. Before he was out of earshot, Sam turned and said, "By the way, the barman knows which one Eddie really is. They say lightning never strikes in the same place twice, but you might want to be careful." And he walked slowly on through the big swing doors that led to the kitchen.

His career as an impromptu Romeo was over and he had begun a new one as a man who hurt. As he crossed the kitchen he couldn't believe the pain that was welling up in his chest. But there was another thing that he knew as well. Another thing about careers coming to an end. The carrot scraping had to stop.

"Chef," he said, coming to a halt by the big steel range. "That was a wonderful meal. If I cut the last ten minutes, it counts as the best time of my life. But it always pays to go out on a high note so I won't be coming back. Ever. Say goodbye to everyone for me. It's not that it hasn't been good here and I hate to leave you in the lurch, but there's something else I need to do. Now. While I still think it matters."

*****

"What else?" asked his father. "What is it that you need to do?"

"I'm not sure yet."

"You're not sure? You've given up your job and you're not sure?"

Sam's father wasn't the sort of man who gave up a job when he wasn't sure. It wasn't how you showed responsibility and raised a family. It was how you hitched a ride to hell in a handcart via drugs and selling your body.

Sam pointed out that he didn't have a family to support, which didn't help much. Nor did a quiet aside, which he was rather hoping his father would miss, about going to London.

"London! *London*! What! You're Dick Whittington now?"

"I have a plan," said Sam.

"What plan? I've been going on at you to plan ahead since you were five years old and you've absolutely refused to listen. Now, suddenly, between yesterday and today you have a plan?"

"It's not exactly a plan," confessed Sam. "More of an idea really. But I've been working on it for, well, longer than you'd believe."

Since the previous evening, in fact, when he'd walked

home from The George - a grown man with tears pricking his eyes, thinking, *Everybody has something.*

"Working on what?" asked his father. "I never see you work outside The George. I don't know how they get you to work *inside* The George. Maybe they don't. Maybe that's why …"

"It's not," said Sam firmly.

"Well what is this you're working on, then? All I ever see you do is draw." His father paused. In his mind's eye there rose the monstrous image of a woman with three breasts and a tail.

"That's right," said Sam. "I'm taking my inner demons to London." And he went upstairs to pack.

His father followed him, making noises, stood on the landing for a while, gave a couple of roars, then came back down to his wife in the kitchen and said, "Can't *you* talk to him?"

"He's grown up now."

"Not very. What the hell's he going to do with a pile of drawings?"

"I expect that's what Nick Park's father said. 'What the hell's he going to do with a pile of plasticine?'" And Sam's mother went upstairs to make sure he took plenty of clean underwear.

His father stood in the middle of the kitchen for a while, then picked up a mop, banged on the ceiling with the handle and shouted, "Who's this Nick Park anyway? Did he accomplish anything playing with plasticine? I think not."

*****

Seven years later, Alice and Eddie were watching late-night TV. Alice couldn't sleep because she was heavily pregnant with twins. Eddie couldn't sleep because she wouldn't let him, even though he got more tired working in a laboratory as a responsible family man than he had done up the Amazon swinging from the vines. Plus the late-night movie reviews weren't really doing it for him. His head was beginning to droop.

"Eddie!"

He leapt guiltily into life.

"It's that chap."

"What chap?"

"The one who pretended to be you. At The George. When you weren't you."

"That's him? Talking to the reviewer? You're sure?"

"Absolutely. It's that movie. The mystical whatsit with computer-generated whatsits. All designed by whosit. Sam. Yes, that's right, Sam Jenkins."

"I thought you said he scraped carrots."

"That's what he told me."

"Well," said Eddie, after a three-minute clip of mystical whatsits. "I didn't see any carrots. I doubt he was just blowing you off."

"You think?"

"Maybe you shouldn't have asked him to have sex with you with such alacrity."

"I thought he was you!"

"He doesn't look anything like me. And you didn't, so you said, talk about anything that remotely applied to me.

In fact, he was a totally different man and yet you wanted to sleep with him."

"I should never have told you that. I can't believe it's rankled with you all these years."

"Well it has to make you wonder."

"Has to make you wonder what?" asked Alice, furiously.

"What exactly was the importance of being Eddie?"

THE SEEING TO

"No, sir!" said Lieutenant Boyd, pink to the gills but determinedly resolute. "I can't do it! Absolutely not!"

"Now you're sure?" asked Major Ellis. "Because this could give you a big career boost."

"Or it could get me court-martialled, sir."

"So could disobeying a direct order," pointed out the major.

"Is it a direct order?" Lt Boyd changed from pink to green, and for a moment the major wondered whether this was the moment to press home his advantage, but he had certain reservations about the lieutenant's ability to get the job done, so he said, "No, of course not. But it *is* a plea from the heart. On behalf of all of us, including the ponies, the golf range and the Christmas turkeys. So be absolutely sure that you can't help before you turn us all down."

"I can't do it, sir," pleaded Lt Boyd. "*Really.* I just can't."

"Fair enough, then. You may go."

Lt Boyd left the second-in-command's office as smartly as he could without actually breaking into a run. Out in the sunshine of the parade square, he took off his beret and flicked sweat from his brow with shaking fingers.

"Jesus, man! You in trouble?" His room-mate, waiting anxiously, was a highly strung youth (for a soldier). He'd been passed over in Major Ellis's search because he obviously didn't have the nerve for the matter in hand.

"No, no, I don't think so." Lt Boyd glanced anxiously back at HQ.

"So, what then?"

"You wouldn't believe it if I told you, which I'm under strict orders not to do."

"Could I guess?"

"Not if you lived *forever*," said Lt Boyd, and he gave an involuntary shudder.

*****

"Well that's that, then," said Major Ellis to the adjutant. "Our last hope. Our *only* hope, in fact. I feel like - who was it? Henry the Eighth? Will nobody rid me of this terrible woman?"

"Henry the Second," corrected Jack Lefevre, an elegant and precious but slightly embittered young Guards captain, who knew he must have dropped a bollock somewhere in his career to have ended up where he was, but couldn't work out how or when. "And it was a priest. A turbulent priest. And I did point out to you that Boyd was too young."

"Well we need somebody young, don't we? Somebody who still has a hard-on for half the day. And that rules me out, I can tell you. With a wife and two teenage daughters climbing the walls in this godforsaken place and the CO bugging me every minute, there's enough angry oestrogen circulating in my vicinity to make sure I never have an erection again!"

Robbie Ellis was a much nicer man than this conversation might suggest. At forty he was a major (overdue lieutenant colonel) from one of the armoured regiments, a good staff officer and, in the normal course of events, a loyal second-in-command. But this wasn't the normal course of events, and Robbie Ellis had something approaching a mutiny on his hands. "God," he said, running his fingers feverishly through his hair, "Is it coming out? It bloody should be."

It wasn't, although it was greying at an impressive rate. It could even have looked rather suave if it hadn't been barbered on a monthly basis by Corporal Flanagan, who was more cut out for topiary work or sheep shearing. But Robbie was really past worrying about what he looked like. There were more fundamental issues at stake - like who was intending to make the ultimate protest by overdosing on the Prozac. Sometimes, when he looked in the mirror, he didn't even recognise himself anymore. His whole world seemed to be turning to base metal. "God!" he said again. "How much longer before I stand a chance of getting out of here?"

"One year, nine months and eighteen days," shouted the chief clerk, who kept track of these things.

"I won't survive that long."

"Yes, you will," said the quartermaster round the door, "because I have the solution." And he came into the office with a flourish, a deus ex machina in a Greek play. "It's Captain Cochrane," he went on. "Christopher Cochrane. And he's coming your way now."

Major Ellis and the adjutant arrived at the window at the same time and struggled silently for the best viewing position.

"He's good-looking," said Robbie, who had won courtesy of his rank.

"He's big," said the adjutant, peering over his head, "which has to be a serious bonus. Who is he anyway? I mean, why is he here?"

"I should know this," said Robbie, brow furrowing, "but I'll have to pass."

"He's a virologist," said the QM. "Actually he's a vet who's just finished a PhD in virology. He's come to work in R and D for six months. Germ warfare stuff. You know, the anti-terrorist initiative."

"He's RAVC then?"

"Yes, but they didn't have anyone regular who was suitable, so they pulled this one in from the TA for a spell."

"How do you know all of this?" asked Robbie. "And why don't I know? I'm the 2IC."

"Yes, but now you just fight about bills for turkeys and I go into the mess and talk to people. *He told me.*"

"He's TA," repeated the adjutant. "So he actually volunteered to come here. Volunteered to come to Bolney. Why? Why would he? He must be mad."

"Big, handsome and mad," said the QM. "Couldn't be better, could he?"

*****

Bolney Camp was in the middle of nowhere - a collection of wooden huts, tin sheds and underground bunkers (most of which were equipped with state-of-the-art laboratories) plus a few squares and crescents of red brick housing surrounded by stunted, slantendicular trees and miles of shooting range. Beyond the ranges, the rolling vastness - a wrap-around horizon of purple moor and granite rocks - was crossed by a single-track road, the only way in or out. Bolney was an elephants' graveyard, the tomb of the mummy, and bad things happened to the careers of people who went there.

The exact details of its military function were never willingly divulged - but broadly speaking it was dedicated to research and development into the methods and consequences of modern warfare. It liaised with Porton Down on NBC matters (i.e., nuclear, biological and chemical warfare) and ran projects of a noisy, dangerous and antisocial nature - rigorously scientific and frighteningly destructive.

In addition to civilian scientists, it was staffed by a wide variety of military personnel from all three services who had been sent there not only because they possessed some particular skill or qualification, but frequently because they were difficult people to send anywhere else. In other words, if a man (or a woman, though much less likely) was peculiarly talented but generally viewed as a "bit of a character", he could find himself on an open-ended posting order heading for three years minimum at Bolney. It wasn't exactly a punishment but it often worked out that way.

Nevertheless, nowhere is distant enough or clandestine enough to escape the attention of a politician in pursuit of financial savings, so in due course Bolney received a visit from a government-sponsored team of management consultants as part of an MOD cost-cutting exercise. Colonel Briggs was the CO at that point – a committed soldier who'd done Iraq and Afghanistan and Iraq again before washing up at Bolney for his final years. And he had little time for self-styled experts with degrees in Business Studies who earned more in a day for pointing out the obvious than soldiers earned in a week for risking their lives. And under circumstances like these Colonel Briggs felt, very powerfully, that it was his job to make sure that the obvious remained hidden. Particularly Sergeant Hoskins and his golf clubs.

Sergeant Hoskins was one of those unusual men who don't feel that they are about to be suffocated in the tight, all-enveloping black rubber of a prototype NBC suit and he would sit quite happily, togged out in the full paraphernalia including breathing tubes, for days and nights on end in the black dark of a bunker, undergoing all manner of deprivations, while scientists did tests on him and took measurements. But once he was out of the suit he liked to practise his golf swing for an hour or so after lunch, and nothing short of being shoved back in the bunker could stop him. Certainly not a government auditing team.

The team had had a rough and unproductive morning in Colonel Briggs' office and they were glad to get out into the fresh air and even gladder, verging on triumphant, when they found Sergeant Hoskins at three o'clock in the afternoon hacking away at lime green golf balls on the sports field. The colonel was annoyed with Hoskins, who'd been warned, but he was even more annoyed that he had felt obliged to try and hide him in the first place. His unit didn't work that way. Didn't and shouldn't. So when the management consultants pointed out to him, as he knew they would, that this man was golfing on government time, his thin veneer of tolerance just split right open.

"And what do you consider army time to be?" he asked.

Eight thirty to five thirty seemed to be the general concensus, although there was one virtuous call for a seven thirty start.

"Those are accountants' hours," said the colonel, scornfully. "Army hours are twenty-four hours a day, seven days a week, fifty-two weeks a year. The army owns these men. If it requires them to get on a troop flight on Christmas Eve and spend the holidays running about on Benbecula or in Kurdistan, then that's what they'll do. And there's no overtime and no negotiation. That's the deal they signed up for. However, in return for this, they are allowed, when nothing is pressing, to play a couple of hours of golf, or fish, or exercise a horse in the middle of the afternoon, or whenever it suits their personal schedules. I don't micromanage - they do the job not the hours, and it runs day and night and bank holiday weekends in this place."

"Well," said the head consultant. "Suppose we leave the time factor out of this for a moment and consider something else. These men are playing this golf, and catching these fish and keeping these horses - and turkeys, for some strange reason - on army land."

"But they live on army land," replied the colonel, slightly puzzled. "They work on army land. They just about *are* army land. Where else would you expect them to do it?"

The leader of the consultancy team wasn't an impatient man. He knew that he had all the gods that mattered on his side, so he said quietly, "Let's put it like this, then. Government land and buildings are being used in this way for private purposes, and possibly private gain, with no remuneration being made and no account being kept."

"But the government has these men's lives," exploded the colonel. "What more does it want? Blood? Oh, yes, I forgot. It's already had that! And no account being kept. Now if you'll excuse me, gentlemen, I have better things to do than talk to people who simply refuse to hear."

In due course the report on Bolney went in - at a cost of tens of thousands of pounds - and the gist of it was this: "Impossible to recommend any specific manpower savings for Bolney Camp because the consultancy team was only privy in the vaguest terms as to what exactly goes on there. However, in respect of the use of army buildings and land, etc., for private purposes, economies could be made (e.g., on maintenance) and remuneration collected (as hire charges, etc.) if a civil servant accountant was attached to the command and the current CO, Colonel Briggs, was replaced by someone more sympathetic to the government's financial position and less attuned to the idiosyncratic requirements of the men."

This report went to the head of the defence audit team, one Henry Pusey, a man of dedication and enterprise when it came to keeping track of government monies and getting himself on the New Year's honours list. After much haranging and some sulking, the army finally replaced Colonel Briggs with Colonel Henrietta Hetherington, an unmarried woman with an unpredictable personality that had been rendered invincible by equal opportunities legislation and fourth-wave feminism. According to her confidential report, she lacked the breadth of vision for progression to brigadier but was of outstanding conscientiousness when it came to supervising minutiae. (Which those skilled in the art of reading military subtext understood to mean that she was stubborn and pernickety and had possibly been overpromoted already.)

*****

Colonel H was a few years on the far side of forty and a big woman. But just to demonstrate that she really was one of the men, she joined a scheduled fitness test two days after her arrival and did it all in the required time - which the PT sergeant put down to intervention from the powers of darkness, because he couldn't see any other way that she could have managed it.

Colonel H was very red and sweaty afterwards and couldn't seem to cool off in spite of a sharp early morning breeze blowing off the Pennines. Acknowledging the hand of the perimenopause in this she announced, to the astonishment of those who had finished before her, that as it could be her lot to be hot and sweaty for some time to come, there was little point in being embarrassed about it. She blew down her singlet and flapped it about a bit to catch the breeze and the PT sergeant read the label sticking out from her bra and it read 38K, which was interpreted in the Sergeants Mess as being a lot bigger than the number 38 on its own could ever suggest. Thirty-eight was the perimeter of the colonel's ribcage in inches, said someone strangely knowledgeable about these things (and who was viewed ever after with a mixture of suspicion and envy), and K was the cup size. Which was the size of the wossnames themselves. And, yes, it had to be one mother of a brassiere and was probably ordered specially off the internet.

So the new colonel turned out to be well-endowed and generally, if healthily, hefty and she wore gold-rimmed specs to read, perched on the end of a very important nose. She had incredible calf muscles and the army shirts were tight around her upper arms but her waist went in surprisingly neatly to the stable belt that held up the regulation barrack dress skirt, and her hair in its thick dark bun was splendid and lustrous when loose, so she wasn't as unattractive as a hundred and sixty pounds and twenty un-partnered years in the army might suggest.

What made her hugely unpopular was her first interview with her second-in-command, Major Robbie Ellis.

"Now," she said, without any preamble, or little pleasantries, or guff about how excited she was to be in command of a unit that could contribute so significantly to the future of modern warfare, "about Corporal Flanagan's Christmas turkeys. The accountant and I have worked out that, for the rent and maintenance of the shed in which he keeps them, we should charge twenty pounds a week. Plus a headage per turkey and some buggeration money for the manure heap, and that comes to ..."

She tossed some figures around and the major caught them and juggled them mentally and said, "One hundred and twenty pounds per turkey, finished weight but that's not oven ready. That's as they stand, with their feathers on. Alive."

"So there's to be the use of an additional shed for slaughtering, plucking and gutting?"

Robbie Ellis made a strangled noise in his throat. "We can't do this, Colonel," he said.

"Can't, Major?" Colonel H looked at him over her gold-rimmed specs, green eyes unclouded by regret or uncertainty. "We must. And it must be done in accordance with regulations, not according to the requirements of the soldiers' Christmas dinners or their wives' housekeeping budgets."

"But ..."

"Don't but me, Major. Not today. I'm really not in the mood to be butted."

"And that was it," said Robbie to the adjutant afterwards. "And not a sodding thing I could do about it. I tried a few times but the accountant is obviously much more influential than I am. And that bloody man, the chief auditor - what's he called? That government fat cat with the 'you don't have to do it that way just because Wellington did' tone of voice."

"Henry Pusey," said the adjutant. "Yes, he frightens her, I suppose. Pension and that, you know. Pity."

Jack Lefevre, coming from a rather grand family, wasn't easily frightened himself. Wasn't easily anything in fact, which made him something of a mixed bag to work with. Sometimes Robbie wished that *he* had the backing of ten thousand insulating acres. On the other hand, he wasn't sure he'd like the responsibility of carrying the name of a family that featured on the Bayeux tapestry. He would, however, have liked the adjutant's thirty-four-inch inside leg, his straight elegant nose (for looking at the colonel down) and his new Range Rover.

"Well Pusey isn't God," he said angrily. "Colonel Briggs cut his own throat in the end by just refusing to cooperate. But new rules are open to interpretation - even negotiation - and that's what any CO with guts will be doing right now. Not giving it all away like this bloody woman. I can't believe it. I don't know what I'm going to say to Corporal Flanagan."

"No," agreed the adjutant, "but I imagine you have a pretty good idea of what he's going to say to you."

*****

"Well, I'll just wring the turkeys' fucking necks now, sir," said Flanagan, "because at that price nobody will be expecting to eat them. They'll be wanting them to live at the bottom of the garden on fresh air and excitement and lay golden fucking eggs."

"Yes, Corporal," said Robbie, "I daresay they will."

There was an awkward pause for a moment or two, then Flanagan brightened suddenly and said, "Maybe I'll wring the accountant's neck!"

"Well, try to hold off on the neck wringing just now," suggested Robbie. "Maybe I'll think of something."

He didn't. He was an inventive and motivated man, but not as motivated as a civil service accountant yoked to a lady colonel who was determined to do in full the job she had been selected to do.

"Now, Major," she said, consulting a Filofax which Robbie longed to get his hands on, just so that he could be prepared occasionally instead of gobsmacked. "Fishing rights on the Bolney river. Let's see … How much is a day on the Test?"

"The Test?" asked Robbie, hoarsely. "Excuse me, ma'am, but I fail to see the comparison. It's very doubtful that there are even any fish in the Bolney. Dead sheep in quantity, I believe, and the odd unexploded shell, but nothing that you'd actually want on your plate at suppertime."

"That's not the point," said Colonel Hetty, tapping her ballpoint impatiently on the desk. Her hands were well manicured and she paused suddenly in her tapping to inspect a nail. "The river is a *facility*. We also have an agreement with DEFRA to keep it maintained, which costs money. So how much for a day on the Test?"

"I have no idea."

"Then find out, Major. And, of course, this brings me to another point. No fishing - no activities other than those pertaining to duty - between the official hours of 7:30 a.m. and 5:30 p.m. I want everybody - *everybody* to be very clear on that. Out of hours activities must be kept *out of hours*."

*****

Everybody in the officers mess longed for Colonel Hetty to develop some out-of-hours activities of her own. The mess at Bolney wasn't splendid, or even particularly harmonious, but it had the only bar you'd want to go into for pushing fifty miles. Unmarried officers lived there, as did those on instructional courses and temporary detachment. Married officers gathered there for lunchtime and pre-dinner drinks - plus meals when their wives were away or had found something better to do than cook (which was so difficult at Bolney that a wife who *had* found something better to do - especially one who had given up a career in the interests of being supportive in the middle of nowhere – was cause for deep unease).

These gatherings, which had been predominantly male and frequently included senior NCOs for serious drinking and poker, were now dominated by Colonel H, who chose not to drink alone in the CO's residence but to invade the mess with her two black Labradors which slavered enthusiastically on the knees of people sitting down and goosed those who were standing up.

She held the floor by virtue of her position, size and a penetrating voice that could have crossed rivers and stopped armies, as indeed it had. She had an opinion on everything and gave it freely, sometimes in Latin, at which she seemed unaccountably expert. Not that anyone else was much of a judge, and with the 38K breasts heaving along to every syllable of "*Cave, cave, deus videt,*" it was easy to be uncritical even whilst you were actually being warned that your behaviour was being monitored. (Unless you were a young artillery officer, in which case you whispered to your mates, "Christ, why doesn't somebody just stick it in her mouth and shut her up?")

Had Colonel Hetty heard this remark, she might just have had the good sense to feign deafness but, by and large, she waded into everyone's conversations, including those specifically designed to repel her, with an inappropriateness that was armour-plated. In short, her social skills were about as well developed as those of a young rhino.

Her feminism, on the other hand, was exceptional. She was as free with information on her menstrual cycle as the quartermaster was about his holidays in Thailand. And it was notable which one of them fared better in the telling. In spite of the fact that the QM went on holiday with the express purpose of getting laid as many times and in as great a variety of ways as he possibly could, he became incoherent with embarrassment on the subject of menstruation and had to be winkled, red and stammering, from behind the bar in order to discuss Colonel Hetty's new proposals for the ecological and economical disposal of sanitary products in the ladies' loos.

Poor Major Ellis, in addition to all his other burdens, was made particularly privy to the vagaries of Colonel H's hormones. Because he was her right-hand man, and because he was a married man with two teenage daughters, and because he had nice sympathetic brown eyes, he was a natural repository for female confidences and one that could be relied upon not to wince or smirk.

Unfortunately, Robbie Ellis, who knew perfectly well that he ought to be above this sort of thing, found himself having to retreat into the corridor to wheeze away some unaccountable and embarrassing hysteria.

"I cannot," he said despairingly to the adjutant, "just cannot cope with discussions about the CO's innards without cracking up. It's terrible. I don't know what comes over me. Some sort of nervous terror, I think. We have an argument about something like ground rent for children's Wendy houses and then she says, 'Don't even think of going against me on this, Major. It's a heavy one this time, so get me two aspirin.' Why does she insist on telling me this stuff?"

"Because you're the only one who will listen," said the adjutant. "When you're not out in the corridor stuffing your hanky in your mouth."

"Doesn't she have a mother?" asked Robbie. "Or a friend? Does anybody visit her? She's lonely. I mean, that's it, isn't it? She's lonely."

"It's called the loneliness of command," said the adjutant, casually flicking back his floppy fair hair. "It's her job. And I, for one, have no intention of being her personal wailing wall."

However, any sympathy that Major Ellis, as the nice man he basically was, could have felt for Colonel Hetty was totally overwhelmed by the exasperating small-mindedness of her accounting. Even the couple of acres of grass that some soldiers had fenced at their own expense for children's ponies had to be charged for as if grass were not a self-renewing resource. The golf range that they had hewn from the moorland over the years and subsequently maintained now had to be hired per person per hour. And this especially irritated Robbie, who had just persuaded his wife to take up the clubs on the off chance that the smell of the heather and the cry of the curlew would penetrate her sulks at finding herself fifteen hundred feet above sea level and sixty miles from a decent hairdresser and enable him to get her kit off more often. Or at all. So far it hadn't worked, and now there was a nice bill sitting on his desk to remind him of how many times the previous month his wife had said, "Not just now, Robbie." She'd given up her job as a schoolteacher, temporarily grateful to escape from increasingly inattentive pupils, but somehow it just wasn't working out.

So Major Ellis watched some of the children's ponies being sold and Lance Corporal Harris's wife's showjumper being shipped back to her father's farm because the shed in which she'd planned to keep it was now going to cost more than a DIY livery yard in Windsor Great Park; and Corporal Harris's wife shipping out after it, because her husband couldn't provide much of a life for her, which was exactly what her father had said at the wedding; and Corporal Harris getting drunk and punching a sergeant on the nose, and getting busted back to private and ruining a promising career; and a pathetic pile of money accumulating in the public fund and being gloated over by a triumphant accountant. And finally Robbie Ellis began to experience the black despair that is born of impotence.

*****

The final straw was Airman James and what became known forever afterwards as "the shagging in the gymnasium".

Soldiers have to be fit, and even the accountants conceded that this was something that could be allowed on government time - which began, at Colonel Hetty's behest, at 7:30 a.m. when she emerged from her own front door to go for a little jog. Rain falls freely on the Pennines and one morning when it was falling more freely than usual she'd obviously decided to go to the camp gym (as the adjutant, who had already heard the story from the chief clerk, who had heard it from the military policeman who had come across Airman James wandering in shock round and round the parade square) explained to Robbie the minute he got to work. Maybe, Jack Lefevre speculated, the colonel had expected to have the gym to herself because she was apparently surprised when it turned out to be occupied by a young airman and a local civilian girl, who worked relief in the cookhouse, locked together in breathless naked contortions on the rubber mats.

Unsure of James's identity at this point, the colonel had bellowed, "Young man! Stand to attention at once!"

Part of Airman James had been at attention for quite some time now, and was determined to stay that way until its job was done, so the lad had to stand starkers with his arms by his side, his heels together, his eyes focused slightly above his CO's head while his penis remained primed and pointed like some heat-seeking missile. "Airman James, ma'am," he mumbled.

"Don't mumble like that, Airman," Colonel H had barked while the girl scrambled desperately for her clothes. "Would you care to tell me what's been going on here?"

James apparently wouldn't. Not because he was being difficult, or even because he wanted to say, "Isn't it bloody obvious?", but because, in the terror of the moment, he couldn't think of a way of putting things that the colonel would find inoffensive.

"Very well then, Airman James. You can explain yourself to Army Legal."

"Army Legal?" Major Ellis was horrified. "Don't you think that's a bit over the top, Colonel?"

"I do not." Colonel H's version of the incident, recounted to Robbie through stiff lips, had been a lot less sympathetic than the adjutant's.

Robbie could see that she was furious. In the interests of Airman James, he backtracked quickly. "But we need to get this one right, don't we, ma'am?" he said carefully. "Don't forget, he's not one of ours. We're dealing with the

RAF here. Now James isn't married or anything, so we have no duty of care in that respect. The girl isn't married, isn't underage and there was no coercion of any sort. So maybe the easiest thing to do would be to RTU James and let the RAF rap him on the knuckles if they feel like it."

"No!" said Colonel H. "This took place in official working hours in direct defiance of my orders."

"OK. Accepted," said Robbie. "So let's look at it this way. Miss Holmes, the girl, wasn't due to start work for twenty minutes, and Airman James *was* in the gym and he *was* exercising. So when you really analyse it, all we have to complain about is the fact that they didn't pay for the use of the rubber mats."

Colonel H knew that her accounting system was hugely unpopular and she knew when she was being got at. "No!" she shouted, bringing both fists down on the desk. "I don't like this and I want an example made. I won't have fornication. It's bad for morale."

Robbie Ellis was even more taken aback than he had been at the start of the conversation. His eyes met his CO's across the desk and for a split second he felt something resonate badly in his subconscious.

"Fornication!" he exploded. "Is that what you call it? Well round here they just call it fucking and I can tell you without a shadow of a doubt that it's bloody marvellous for morale!"

There was a silence that clanged like a fire alarm before Colonel H said in a dangerous voice, "Would you like to be RTU'd as well, Major?"

Robbie sighed and ran a hand that shook slightly through his hair.

"Oh, come on, Colonel Hetty," he said, after a couple of deep breaths. "Let's be reasonable about all of this. Let the lad off with a warning or a fine. He's only nineteen, for chrissakes."

The CO straightened her gorgets with a hand that was a lot steadier than her second-in-command's. "Don't call me Hetty, Major. *Ever.* You're dismissed."

*****

Robbie Ellis crossed the parade square at 6:00 p.m. and went into the mess for a drink because the colonel, unusually, hadn't and he needed one. Badly.

"Well," said the adjutant, handing him a glass of whisky. "You may or may not be pleased to hear that the gymnasium incident wasn't the only disaster of the day."

Robbie flopped into a leather club chair and rubbed his forehead wearily. Normally, he had a high colour which went well with his gunmetal hair, but now he looked pale and there was an uncharacteristic dullness in his eyes. The adjutant, on the other hand, who normally looked bored, now seemed faintly animated. "It's Sergeant Hoskins," he went on. "He's broken out of the bunker. He seems to have finally decided that living underground in a rubber onesie and a gas mask twenty-four seven for a month on the trot, while being fed nerve gas pills and sustaining multiple venopunctures, is over and above the call of duty. For a man whose official hours are seven thirty to five thirty."

"And you have to give it to him," he added, going behind the bar, opening the fridge, picking out his bottle of champagne, which was bunged with a silver stopper between times, and pouring himself a glass. "The chap's timing is immaculate. A collaborative visit from some other NATO scientists and suddenly he's pulling out tubes and peeling off rubber. Buggered things up spectacularly. He intends, I believe, to protest to Director Equipment Capability Special Projects in Whitehall that this place is tearing the arse out of it."

"Claim custom and practice, in other words," said Robbie. "Play them at their own game."

"Exactly."

"And if he wins, the government will lose financially because now they'll need three Sergeant Hoskins to do the same job. In fact, they'll need three of everybody to do everything. And all for a few hours of golf." Robbie took a swig of the whisky, which burnt his throat, and the adjutant pointed to the label on the bottle and winced. "Of course, Hoskins' career will be over whatever happens," he added when he'd recovered his voice. "He'll put himself between a rock and a hard place."

He spoke calmly enough but he knew that he was looking at yet another can of worms that would be spilling all over his desk by lunchtime the next day. And he felt sick at the thought. He also knew that for Hoskins' sake he had to talk him out of this particular approach. Persuade him to pass the day's incident off as unusual stress. Then he had to control the CO, stop her from taking it all as a personal insult, persuade her to review the scientific schedules and arrange for them to be adjusted. And all of this while she was still in a towering rage with him over fornication versus fucking (he had no idea what had come over him there} and probably planning to terminate his career.

"Jack," he said to the adjutant, "I wish I was a little rabbit forty feet under the ground."

"Interesting concept," said the adjutant, holding his glass up to the light and squinting at the bubbles. "A serious collapse of morale there, I think. And no wonder. Of all the commanding officers I've ever known, even by reputation, none of them, including the homicidal McFadden, could compete at the art of taking the joy out of life with this repellent female."

Robbie stood up and went to the bar for another whisky. Other people were beginning to trickle in now and the young artillery officer, with his customary frankness, said, "Miserable old dyke."

Robbie didn't answer and nobody else found this a thought-provoking remark, not beyond silent agreement anyway, except for a balding, bespectacled officer who was rummaging around for ice. Avuncular and rather country in polished veldtschoens, his remaining sandy hair clashing with the maroon woolly pully of the Royal Army Medical Corps. Lieutenant Colonel Mac Macdonald chewed it over for a while and then said, "She may be miserable but she's certainly not a dyke."

Lt Col Mac was a doctor but not the doctor who dealt with the CO's health so he didn't feel badly about discussing her. He was in fact a neurosurgeon, whose job at Bolney was to shoot monkeys in the head in order to study brain damage. His conscience cried out every time he picked up their limp little paws but he'd watched young soldiers dying of cerebral oedema that he'd been helpless to alleviate, so he'd made his choice and bore it as best as he could - with a lot of whisky and plenty of ice.

"So, Doctor," said the adjutant, taking out his swizzle stick and dispersing champagne bubbles with it. "Tell us about the colonel's overpowering heterosexuality. Pretend we care."

"Well," began Lt Col Mac, who was married to an ex-psychiatric nurse, "I have no insider knowledge, you know, but I suspect that she draws attention to her menstrual cycle so frequently because she wants to remind us that she's a woman. She needs, in her position, to be as commanding as a man but she doesn't want to be thought of as one. She's also, in this way," he held up a hand to stifle the young artillery officer, who was developing something even ruder to say on the subject, "drawing our attention to the fact that she is still relatively young and still technically fertile. What she may want, in fact, is a lover. Perhaps," he held up his hand again, "I should say *needs*, because she may be totally unaware of this at a conscious level."

"Me too," said the adjutant. "I've certainly never put the CO and lover together in the same thought, I can assure you."

"And her persnicketiness over government guidelines,"

went on Lt Col Mac, "is an exaggerated form of a woman's greater conscientiousness and greater inclination to respect authority. Her career is all that Colonel Hetty has, so naturally she's not going to lay it on the line for everybody else's benefit."

"She doesn't have to lay it on the line," said the adjutant. "She just has to stand up and argue a point occasionally."

"Well," the doctor in Lt Col Mac was obviously giving this some thought, "maybe if somebody fulfilled her needs, she'd be less manic about fulfilling the needs of the government auditors. Or at least distracted from them."

"So what she needs is a good seeing-to," said the young artillery officer.

"It's an expression I'd prefer to avoid," replied Mac, "meaning, as it does, that if a man can't dominate in one way then he'll do it in another. I believe the very idea would now come under the banner of toxic masculinity. But since I prefer to think that none of us here would want to be deliberately toxic we can take it in this instance to mean, would Colonel Hetty be happier and more relaxed and get off our backs a bit if she had a nice lover, then I'd have to say 'yes.' The desire for sex is a basic requirement of the id, whoever you are. And," he added, poking at his ice (he'd found a bottle of Glenfiddich, Robbie noticed), "I'd put money on the fact that if she'd been post-orgasmic when she went into the gym this morning, she'd have just turned round and come out again. Given Airman James a rocket later and then forgotten about it. And James would have been more careful in future and a good lad wouldn't have had his career blighted before it even got started."

"A nice lover," said Robbie thoughtfully. "Where the hell would we find one of those? And how could we keep finding them?"

"You wouldn t have to," said the doctor. "Only the first one. Once she'd got the hang of things, she'd start finding her own."

"Hard to imagine that," said the adjutant. "On this planet, anyway."

"Maybe, when you're just twenty-six years old," Colonel Mac looked reflective, "but from where I'm standing, Colonel Hetty isn't unattractive."

"And don't forget the allure of a uniform," pointed out the QM, who had found the entire discourse riveting. "Disciplinary fantasies and all that. Like going to a dominatrix."

"You frighten me sometimes," said Robbie, but in truth the idea of getting Colonel Hetty a lover who would distract and soften and mitigate had taken tentative root in his desperate breast. "So he has to be nice," he repeated thoughtfully. "Jesus, that's a big one."

"And unattached because the CO has a duty of care and can't fornicate, as she puts it, with somebody else's partner," added the adjutant, drawn in spite of himself. "And it has to be an officer or it would be fraternisation. Even then it's dicey because he'd be under her command and she's a stickler for rules. But these things do go on so let's think - this is Bolney, after all. There are always a few uncommitted oddball officers in this place."

"I think we need somebody sane," interrupted Lt Col Mac, "or partially so."

"I meant uncommitted in the sense of not having a partner."

"Right."

"So somebody relatively sane and single, who still remembers how to do it," mused Robbie.

"Somebody young?"

"But not so young that Colonel Hetty feels she ought to be breastfeeding him instead," Lt Col Mac pointed out. "And he has to look as if he cares, or it won't work at all."

"Well, it's getting harder by the minute, isn't it?" said the adjutant. "What with the stickler for rules bit and the fact that he's going to need a lot of something or other to get her to overlook them … How about you?"

All eyes swivelled to the quartermaster.

Robbie Ellis thought that an idea worth spinning. "You're not young but you probably have more sex in a fortnight in Thailand than most married men can wheedle out of a wife in a year. You should be pretty slick."

The QM was in his forties and had been going to Thailand ever since it had become a cheap enough holiday destination to appeal to his mercenary spirit. He'd never been married, or even come close, and maybe that was why he was sufficiently worried about male pattern baldness to keep combing his hair to cover the inroads it was making on his once well-covered scalp. He had a biggish nose and a chin that was slate blue even at breakfast, and he could have been handsome once but nobody present had known him then. To most minds the best thing he had going for him (apart from lubricious holiday reports) was a willingness to recognise his own limitations.

"Yes, well," he said now, "don't forget that in Thailand I pay for it. I don't think offering Colonel H a few American dollars is going to cut it."

"So you couldn't seduce her, then?" asked Robbie.

"Why do you think I go to Thailand?"

"Because you're a charmless bugger who couldn't talk a woman out of a burning car?" suggested the adjutant.

The QM shrugged. "You said it."

"I'm single and youngish," remarked someone, reflectively. He was slim and smallish and nobody noticed him much.

"Yes, but you're probably gay."

"Probably, but I don't know for sure."

"Well if you don't know for sure after five years in the SAS, which is a brigade of shirt lifters if anything ever was, then I shouldn't think embarking on a campaign to get Colonel Hetty into bed is the way to find out," said the adjutant.

"It might be."

"Let's get back to you on it," said Robbie. "But in the meantime, if you have a Road to Damascus experience with a woman don't forget to let us know. Now, who else is there?"

"Tony Evans."

"Too boring."

"Tom Hunt."

"Too slow."

"Keith Davidson."

"Too stupid. The CO's bright. Not our idea of bright perhaps, but she likes to talk."

"Maybe, we ought to move on to the boffins. Do they talk or do they just think?"

"A lot of the boffins are civvies. We must keep it in house," said Robbie.

"Captain Devlin, that cavalry chap staying here for the tank trials. He's bright, he went to Eton," said the QM.

"Not the best provenance for a convincing heterosexual predator," said the adjutant. "We may need to give him a map."

"Christ, no," exclaimed the SAS officer. "There's nothing more lethal than a cavalry officer with a map."

"God, if only we had some foreigners here at the moment," said Robbie. "A Frenchman or an Italian or a Spaniard ... A touch of the continental *je ne sais quoi* might have been just the thing."

"An African would be good," said the QM. "Colonel Hetty was there for a bit, you know. Some big black man offered the quartermaster twelve cows for her."

"Was that on a weight for weight basis?"

"Lieutenant Boyd. Andy Boyd," suggested the young artillery officer who had been hastily fabricating a fiancée for himself.

"Young," said Robbie Ellis, brightening a little. "Barely older than you. But near, very near. We could sound him out. Who's going to do that?"

"You, of course," said the QM.

"Oh, shit. What am I supposed to say?"

"You'll think of something."

*****

And, of course, he had. But nothing that could overcome the terror that had gripped the young lieutenant at the mere mention of Colonel Hetty, let alone the concept of trying to get her out of her clothes. In fact, Lieutenant Boyd's reaction was such that Robbie, now presented with Captain Christopher Cochrane by an excited QM, and grappling with the adjutant at the HQ office windows in order to get a good look at him, was inclined to be less hopeful than he would have been thirty minutes previously.

However, he thought, watching Cochrane come across the parade square, this guy must have been a student for what? Five years veterinary degree, three or four years postgraduate research - pushing nine years in a university environment. He must have got into bed with all sorts in that time. Robbie himself, having gone straight from a minor, single-sex public school to Sandhurst, had missed out on a government-sponsored education in cannabis and condoms, but Christopher Cochrane, as the QM kept pointing out, must have experienced the equivalent of nine years in Thailand. A sexual marathon that must have equipped him for anything. Either that or he simply had an enormous forebrain and no balls.

He was certainly good-looking - tall, broad, curling dark hair a little farther down the neck than it ought to have been. But Robbie wasn't complaining. He could see the advantage of a touch of independence. And now that Captain Cochrane was pretty well in the room with them he could appreciate his rather striking blue eyes.

"So you've come to see the CO?" he asked, looking right into them as Captain Cochrane saluted in that rather laconic way that officers with a professional qualification rather than a full Sandhurst training seemed to effect. "She's just along the corridor. Expecting you, I presume?"

"She is," said Captain Cochrane with a charming smile.

So far the word "sir" hadn't passed his lips. All to the good, thought Major Ellis, tolerantly. An obvious level of casual self-confidence, at ease but not offhand, polite but not conscious of authority. And TA not regular, so that neither his career nor, by extension, his future depended on Colonel Hetty's opinion of him.

All very positive, Robbie thought. A state of affairs that meant the rules weren't *really* getting bent. This could be the man to ease the endless uphill struggle that had become his life. But why should Cochrane cooperate?

He turned to the QM when Cochrane had gone into the CO's office and put this to him. "He's got no long-term interest in this place," he said, "and he's hardly likely to take an enormous fancy to her, so why should he do it?"

"We bribe him," said the QM.

"Bribe him?" Robbie was shocked. "What the hell with?"

"Ah, well." The QM leaned forward and smiled conspiratorially. It made him look exactly like someone who used Superdrug Colour for Men before his dirty fortnights in Thailand.

"Amaze me," said Robbie.

"Cochrane's doing this six months here, right? But basically he's sick of research and wants to start up his own veterinary practice. And what do you need for that?"

"Animals?"

"Equipment! Equipment exactly like the stuff we've written off by the ton in this place: X-ray machines, ultrasounds, thermographs, anaesthetic machines … you name it."

"And you think we could give him this stuff?"

"Yes!"

"Well, you have amazed me," said Robbie, sitting down suddenly. "Not least because quartermasters won't normally give you the steam off their shit, and you've never been a notable exception. You had a visit from the ghost of Christmas future or something?"

"I have," replied the QM grimly. "And the fucker's an accountant. The CO is cutting these guys far too much slack. She needs to be fed some revolutionary pillow talk."

"Would out-of-date equipment be any good to Cochrane?" asked the adjutant, completely undisturbed by talk of serious pilfering.

"It's only out-of-date for cutting-edge research, not for ordinary use. And some of it's never even been used - taken so long in the pipeline it was OBE before it even got here."

"Never been used," repeated Robbie. "That's quartermaster wet dream country, isn't it? The stuff you put in a trophy cupboard and take on with you to the great quartermaster's store in the sky."

"Yep," nodded the QM, "and there's only me even remembers it's down there, at the back of some unused bunkers. The boffins don't keep track as long as they have what they need at the moment. Keeping track is my job. In any case, as I said, some is already written off, anything additional could become BEM. Beyond economic repair. Removed from the books. It would cease to exist."

"And nobody knows about it? *Nobody*?'

"No. In any case we'd hardly make a dent in what's down there. Sounds perfect, doesn't it?"

"Sounds like 'Straight to Colchester Jail,'" said Robbie. "'Do not pass 'Go' and do not pause to collect surplus army equipment.' I'll think about it."

*****

The next day he had Airman James in his office, tears running down handsome cheeks that looked as if they'd barely seen a razor. James's terror of Army Legal was slightly less than the shame he was going to feel at having to tell his mother that he'd failed in his chosen career before he'd really started. And why. The implication was that suicide looked preferable. And through it all Colonel H sat as massive and heartless as an Easter Island statue.

And then there was Sergeant Hoskins - in an interview conducted behind the CO's back this time - determined to proceed to DEC(SP).

"Don't do this in the belief that you can stay in the army afterwards," hissed Robbie, "because you can't. If you do, you'll die here. Believe me. They'll *never* move you. There'll be no promotion. And no bloody afternoons of golf, either. You'll be in that bunker seven thirty to five thirty *forever*."

But Sergeant Hoskins, for whom trying to change course by pleading stress was tantamount to confessing to cowardice or impotence, was not to be persuaded.

"Think about it, Dick," begged Robbie. "*Please.* I have no axe to grind. In fact, it'll make my job easier if you go down to Whitehall this very afternoon and get it over with. But in a few years' time, somebody will be scraping you off the bunker walls and saying, 'Who is this guy and who the hell gave him a gun?'"

By lunchtime he was tearing his hair out. "I've thought about it," he hissed to the QM. "We'll try it."

"So how are we going to put it exactly?" he asked in a low voice as he and the QM and the adjutant sat closeted in his office that evening.

"Remind us how you put it to Andy Boyd," said the adjutant. This was the first thing that had fully engaged his attention since he'd arrived.

"I asked him to seduce the CO," said Robbie. "In retrospect, I think it was a bit direct. I should have warmed up to it somehow. For a full five minutes, I thought he was actually going to faint."

"I think we interest Cochrane in the equipment first," said the QM, whose mercenary streak mostly dictated his own actions.

"You could be right," said Robbie. "Get him fantasising about a fully equipped, loan-free veterinary practice and then try to interrelate it to a fantasy about getting into bed with the colonel."

"A nightmare, you mean," said the adjutant. "A nightmare about getting into bed with the colonel. Let's face it, there's no way we can paint that pretty. It's a transaction. Present it as such. He's got a professional qualification, he's bound to be a tradesman at heart."

"I think maybe he's right," said the QM.

"Unkind but right," said Robbie. "How did your family make its money, Jack?"

"Mostly we committed murder," replied the adjutant. "Killed for it. But that was a long time ago, when you were allowed to. And got given castles afterwards. But seducing someone for an X-ray machine? Now *that's* trade."

"In fact," said Robbie, "it would actually be a miracle. It may be a more feasible proposition to slowly poison her. We could count on you for that, couldn't we?"

"No question about it," agreed the adjutant.

"You're joking, right?" The QM had joined the army as a boy soldier, with no qualification other than a remarkable tolerance for being shouted at. He had risen through the ranks of ordnance and logistics and acquired a fine grasp on how to equip and move a military force but none at all on irony, sarcasm or the milder forms of leg-pulling.

"Barely," said Robbie. The trouble with Bolney, he thought, was that one had to totally recalibrate one's idea of sanity. If any of this had occurred to him a year ago he would have been sure that he was becoming clinically unravelled.

*****

The three of them cornered Christopher Cochrane about a week later at eleven thirty one night when he was slumped in a mess armchair with a beer balanced on his chest, watching a late movie on the TV. He'd been in a laboratory, they knew, till nineish but he didn't seem in a hurry to go to bed. And he didn't look as if it was because he was too tense to sleep.

As the three of them came in he gave them a half-smile and waggled the fingers that were wrapped round the beer bottle. No glass.

"Don't bother to get up," said the adjutant, rather too pleasantly.

Captain Cochrane eased himself a little straighter in the chair.

"No, really," said the adjutant. "Obviously, it's an effort."

"Jack!" hissed Robbie. "Let's not antagonise him from the outset."

"Just trying to see if a week or two of regular has got him intimidated by authority," whispered the adjutant. "We'll take this as a 'no', shall we?"

"Sorry," said Christopher Cochrane with a grin. "I'm still in uniform, right? Supposed to get up and click my heels or something?"

"Something," said Robbie Ellis, "but let's not worry about that now. We've got a proposition to put to you. Perhaps we should all have a drink." He turned to the QM. "You fix them, Q. Put them on Jack's tab. It's time he started giving something back to the proletariat."

"Now, Christopher …" he began, with an encouraging smile.

"Well," said Cochrane, about twenty minutes later. "If this doesn't beat all. My friends thought I must be mad to want to join the TA and play at soldiers but I told them it would be a laugh. Seduce the colonel, eh? Ignore the fact that she'll probably be as receptive as a female grizzly that isn't in heat, and just go ahead and get the job done - several times - until she becomes putty in all of our hands. And for this I get ... what is it? An anaesthetic machine that I won't even see until after it could have been the most use to me?" He grinned cheerfully at them.

"Not just an anaesthetic machine," protested the QM, recklessly itemising equipment on his fingers until he'd used up both hands.

"Do you think we're mad?" asked Robbie.

"I think you're desperate," said Cochrane. "I think it's me that's mad for taking you seriously."

"So you are taking us seriously?"

"I'm taking the managers of Barclays Bank seriously," said Cochrane. "Particularly their interest rates."

He was a bit of a mixture, this chap, thought Robbie. But a convenient mixture. Still student enough to view the seduction of Colonel Hetty much as he would a particularly tasteless rag stunt, but man enough to have a deep appreciation of debt and how nice it would be to start a new career without being up to his neck in it.

"So the question is," said Cochrane, thoughtfully rubbing his chin which was inclined to un-officer-like stubble, "am I prepared to prostitute myself?"

"Now don't look at it like that," protested Robbie.

"Look at it from the philanthropic angle - that you're trying to help the careers, the home life and the sanity of any number of good men and women. Especially me."

"The philosophers call it utilitarianism," added the adjutant. "Which means that the morally right action in any circumstance is the one that will bring about the greatest total or aggregate happiness."

"How the hell did you get to be so smart, Jack?" asked Robbie. "You certainly weren't bred for it."

There was a silence after this, during which Cochrane ostensibly went back to the movie, legs stretched out, hands behind his head. His eyes followed the action but Robbie hoped that his thoughts were elsewhere. The adjutant, whom the QM had provided with a pink gin, went off to the bar to tip it out and get some champagne.

"She's big, isn't she?" said Cochrane suddenly.

"Received wisdom has it that size doesn't matter," replied Robbie.

"She's old."

"Well if she was twenty-one and looked like Scarlett Johansson we'd have been killed in the fucking rush, wouldn't we?" said the QM. "Not standing here pleading with you."

"This equipment," said Cochrane. "That's all above board, is it?"

"Oh, absolutely," said Robbie and the QM in unison.

"But keep it under your hat," added the QM. "This is not a thing we want broadcast for obvious reasons. So mum's the word."

"But the equipment would be legal and everything?"

"Totally."

"I don't know." Cochrane gave a sudden laugh and ran his hands through his hair. "Too long?" He caught the adjutant, who had returned with his champagne, looking thoughtfully at him.

"Leave it," said the adjutant. "It gives you that Hollywood antihero look that's so mind-numbingly effective with women."

"And if she isn't numbed?"

"The doctor said she was secretly gagging for it," the QM reminded him.

"All you have to do is tap into her subconscious," added Robbie.

"So I'm a hypnotist now?"

"A catalyst," suggested the adjutant.

"Yeah, well." Cochrane laughed again. "The trouble with catalysts is that the chemical reactions they're involved in can frequently run either way. Is this an all or nothing deal or do I get points for trying?"

"You certainly do, my son," said the QM, patting him on the shoulder. "I'll grade you on a curve, and the more details you give me the steeper the curve gets. Now don't forget the dogs. They're your intro. What could be easier for a vet?"

*****

Captain Cochrane, having finally agreed to the seduction of Colonel Hetty, didn't waste any time. When she popped into the mess the following evening for what she called an aperitif, he immediately got stuck into the Labradors, which everyone else was carefully avoiding because they'd obviously just rolled in cowpats.

It was noble work, Robbie and the adjutant agreed, especially for a man who had to do his own laundry. Certainly, it seemed to make Colonel Hetty very jolly. She had changed into civvies and was wearing a flowing skirt that uncharitably didn't start to flow until it had clung like a wet T-shirt to her ample bottom, and a silk blouse that, even with the top button undone, was struggling to accommodate the 38Ks. To give him credit, Cochrane didn't glance at them once. He was easy and obviously entertaining, and he had a killer smile that Robbie wanted to borrow and try on his wife.

"Does he look to you like he's slept with a lot of women, Jack?" Robbie whispered.

"God knows," replied the adjutant. "How does that look?"

"Like me," said the QM.

"Shit."

Colonel Hetty was getting quite frisky now. "A vet!" she shouted across to them at one point. "That's a change, isn't it? Long arms, you see, for calving cows." And she held up one of Cochrane's and waggled it around playfully. Casually brawny as it was, she manhandled it with ease.

"Oh, God," said the QM. "Just imagine how far ..."

"No," said Robbie hastily. "Do *not* go there."

At this point the mess manager announced dinner, and

Colonel Hetty took her leave in order to be the guest of honour at a wives' club evening. Robbie fervently hoped his own wife was going. Did women get dressed up that much for other women? Could a woman sulk for fifteen months on end? And was it all about a disrupted career, two teenage girls who grumbled when they had to go to boarding school and grumbled when they had to come home, and a view out of the kitchen window that consisted of two dead trees, five miles of tussocky grass and a staggered line of targets for anti-tank guns?

"Well," said the adjutant to Cochrane as the three of them closed round him on the way to the dining room. "Seems like you were doing pretty well with the CO there. She looked riveted. What were you talking about?"

"Anal glands."

"Anuses?" The adjutant blanched visibly.

"Anal *glands*. The two little sacs either side of a dog's anus. When the dog defaecates these little glands empty into the droppings and do a scent marking job but sometimes - when the diet is incorrect, say - they don't empty properly and then they get distended and sore, and even infected and full of pus, so you have to put your finger into the dog's anus …"

"*Please*," said Robbie, covering his ears. "We're just about to have dinner."

"Christ," said the adjutant, weakly. "You're supposed to be chatting her up, and frankly I think we'll be very lucky if she doesn't just vomit all over you."

Cochrane laughed. "It's fine," he said. "Doggy owner

talk. The doggy owner version of discussing the latest movie. Trust me, we're bonding."

"Over dogs' arseholes?" said the QM, shaking his head in amazement. "No wonder I never made any headway with the women in this country. I was obviously going about it all wrong."

*****

Captain Cochrane pursued the advantage that he had opened up by dint of his peculiar veterinary knowledge and amazing tolerance for being smeared in cowshit, and to everyone's delight managed to persuade Colonel Hetty, in a very casual and platonic way as he explained later, to accompany him to a local agricultural show, which he'd intended to visit anyway, in order to see the cows, sheep, horses and, of course, dogs, which he liked, as opposed to MOD boffins and their lethal viruses, which he was rather going off.

But the advantage, he added, of working with such cuties as Ebola, Hanta and some terrifying descendant of the Spanish Lady was that they made Colonel Hetty seem quite harmless.

He took the colonel in his car, which Robbie Ellis watched from the window of his quarter and approved of because it meant that the CO wasn't in charge for once.

It was a successful expedition, Cochrane reported the following week. Colonel Hetty seemed to have been relaxed with him because he wasn't a full-time soldier and as such had no requirement for a spectacular confidential report or, indeed, any other endorsement from her. That was the impression he'd received, he said, plus she'd been quite giggly on occasions, though no mention of her oestrous, sorry, *menstrual* cycle at all. Which, based on what he'd heard, was perhaps unusually coy of her.

Robbie Ellis and the adjutant looked at each other. Was this a good sign?

"What's coy?" asked the QM.

"Is it time for a real date, do you think?" asked Robbie.

"Or just try and catch her in the gym?" suggested the adjutant.

"And then bill her for the use of the rubber mats," finished Robbie. "OK, Jack, very funny."

"No," said Cochrane, who wasn't in a position to understand the allusion but had grasped the implications. "It's a point. It means, do I do it formally or informally?"

"Well, if it were me," said Robbie, "and you may think this is cowardly, I wouldn't go for grabbing her behind the bicycle sheds, or in any other location where she might feel like putting up a fight if you happen to have misread the signs. At least if you ask her for a date you'll know, in principle at least, whether or not she's interested."

"We'll organise the date," he went on, when there'd been agreement to this approach, "a good restaurant, if we can find one that isn't a million miles away and booked well into the next decade, and underwrite it financially. All you have to do is pick an appropriate moment in the next week and ask her."

"Well," said Cochrane, "thank God I got the easy bit."

*****

He gave them an anxious few days while he apparently weighed up and chatted up Colonel Hetty for a while longer and then, just when they'd decided he was turning chicken, he put his head round Robbie's office door and whispered, "Seven thirty next Saturday night."

And that was it.

Colonel Hetty and he left the camp separately, a subterfuge which seemed encouraging, but Colonel Hetty come back to her quarter alone, which Robbie watched with mixed feelings.

The following day there was a curry lunch in the mess - something of a tradition in army circles and one that made wives, who could often think of a lot better things to do on Sundays, complain and groan all the way there. Of course Bolney wasn't rich in alternatives but, even so, Robbie found himself going alone. As second-in-command he felt it was his duty to attend and be sociable. Plus, there was the prospect of a bulletin from Cochrane.

He was having a drink with the adjutant and the QM in one of the quieter anterooms when Lt Col Mac, the doctor, came in.

"So," he said, "I see you're following my prescription for a new and improved Colonel Hetty." He paused for a moment. "It was rather spurious, you know. Mostly a joke."

"Oh, that." Robbie forced a laugh. He was wearing a new pink striped shirt, which he'd thought might appeal to his wife, but the collar was tighter than it should have been and so the laugh sounded rather strangled. The penalties of catalogue shopping, as his wife had pointed out to him, right before she'd said that she wasn't coming to the lunch. And that pink wasn't his colour. "Oh, that," he repeated. "That conversation in the mess? Well, of course it was a joke. I finally let Andy Boyd in on it last week. Apparently he was still wetting his pants over it."

"But now it isn't," said the doctor.

"Sorry?"

"I was at the agricultural show last week."

"So the veldtschoens are for real, then?" remarked the adjutant, who was also wearing a pink shirt but, having hand-picked it at Turnbull and Asser, he'd got the shade and fit just so. Plus he was blond and young and tanned, not going grey and grey-faced from overwork and anxiety.

"I saw Christopher Cochrane and the CO there," went on the doctor, who knew Cochrane from the bunkers. "It didn't strike me as a natural pairing, although I must give credit, the colonel looked as if it had struck her exactly like that. As far as it had gone. Which is how far, exactly?"

Robbie put a finger to his lips.

The doctor lowered his voice. "What happens if it backfires badly?"

"Frankly, things couldn't be much worse," said Robbie. "Unless the CO finds out that the whole thing has been a set-up. Which she won't if *all* of us are careful and keep our mouths shut."

"OK," said the doctor, running fingers through his sandy hair and casting surreptitious glances around. "But it would be better if it succeeded, wouldn't it? Have you advised Cochrane at all?"

"Advised him?"

"About mature women."

"Don't look at me," said the adjutant.

"Or me," added the QM hastily, in case anyone thought he went all the way to Thailand, paid for it, and still got stuck with ones who were past their "best before" date.

"About their special requirements," Mac explained.

Special requirements, thought Robbie. Mature women were special needs persons now? In what way? Could this be where he was going wrong? "Cochrane's a medical man," he said vaguely.

"He's a *vet*," said the doctor in exasperated tones.

"And animals don't get old?"

Mac snorted.

"Lunch, gentlemen, please," shouted the mess manager.

Robbie and the adjutant settled themselves either side of Christopher Cochrane, who was staring into a plate of curry. As they sat down he glanced from pink shirt to pink shirt and said, "Hello, girls."

"They're very confident in their masculinity," said Lt Col Mac who was not to be shaken off in this enterprise. Dragging up a chair, he jockeyed for position with the QM.

"Must be," said Cochrane, who was wearing a black corduroy shirt and jeans. He had not yet learned that there was casual and then there was army casual. What he was wearing was actually "scruff order" but he didn't seem concerned, except with the curry. "What's this?" he asked, holding up a piece of petrified matter.

"Bombay duck," said the QM. "But never mind the

food. How did it go last night? Dish the dirt, my son. And remember that the curve is as yet unplotted. You're looking at a blank piece of paper and I'm the man with the pencil."

"Well," said Cochrane, holding the Bombay duck up to the light for scientific inspection. "It's fish, right?"

"Forget the bloody food, will you?"

"Yes, OK. Well, it wasn't as easy as the agricultural show. More one-on-one, you know. Not as many distractions or as many obvious conversation pieces. Plus it was on a different footing, which seemed to disconcert her a bit. Actually made her a bit quiet. Certainly she avoided talking about work, except the details of my research, maybe ..."

"Didn't want to emphasise her role as CO," interrupted the doctor. "That's a good sign. She wants to keep on an even footing so as not to frighten you away."

"Mm," said Cochrane.

"Give me that!" said the QM irritably, snatching at the Bombay duck.

"I'm probably going to regret this question," said the adjutant, "but what *did* you talk about?"

"Pyometra in the unspeyed bitch."

"What?"

"Septic wombs."

"Well, she must have loved that."

"It interested her."

"Anything else?"

"Mammary tumours."

"In English?"

"Breast lumps," supplied the doctor.

"In Colonel Hetty's breasts?" asked the QM, hopefully.

"No," said Cochrane. "In the Labradors'."

"Well I'm pleased I subbed you for a bottle of Bollie so you could talk about doggy breast lumps all night," said the adjutant, morosely.

"Did you snog her?" asked the QM.

"Snog?" repeated Robbie with a faint start. "What sort of word is that for a grown man?"

It didn't seem to bother Cochrane. "No, I didn't," he said. "I'm going a bit carefully here, considering what's at stake. I've never dated a forty-odd-year-old before. She might operate on a totally different timescale from me. As well as living on one."

The doctor looked significantly at Robbie, who then felt that he ought to come up with something that could be roughly construed as guidance, so he said, "Well, let's see now, what sort of time scale do you operate on?"

Cochrane shrugged. "Anything from two hours upwards."

"And that two hours would be what, exactly?"

"The length of time from meeting to getting into bed."

Two hours, thought Robbie. *Two fucking hours?* The previous evening, he'd spent three more hideously expensive hours out on the golf range with a wife of nearly twenty years standing; putting his arms round her to help her swing, pointing out the rosiness of the sunset and the softness of the moss, and he'd got absolutely bloody nowhere. A six-course banquet of nothing followed by a scoop of sod all.

"Two hours," repeated Lt Col Mac. "And the outside timescale would be what?"

"Twenty-four hours. Forty-eight tops."

The adjutant put down his fork. This Colonel Hetty business was turning out to be more thought-provoking than a guy seized with habitual ennui was really comfortable with. He had a pretty "made in Chelsea" fiancée back in London, and he'd been putting the fact that she'd been less than ecstatic with him of late down to this horrible Bolney Camp hiccough in his career. But now he was beginning to wonder. She had dogs. *He* had dogs, but he'd thought they were just for fetching pheasants and he didn't have them up on the bed like she did. Maybe he ought to take them more seriously. Talk to Cochrane about them. Get fluent in this septic womb speak.

A long silence ensued during which Cochrane forked up his curry and then stood up. "Look, I'll get it done," he said. "I just can't court by committee like this. Leave me alone and just wait for the results. If there are any. OK?"

And he walked away to pick up his pudding which, this being a buffet, he elected to eat alongside somebody else.

"The nerve of him!" said the QM furiously.

"Well," the adjutant poked absently at his cooling food, "we picked him for his nerve."

"Where *is* the CO anyway?" asked Mac.

"She was supposed to be here," said Robbie.

"So why isn't she?"

"I don't know," replied Robbie. "And frankly, Scarlett," he flicked the doctor's red tie, "I don't give a damn."

But Lt Col Mac felt anxious. The Hippocratic oath was nagging at him. First, do no harm. But he now felt that he'd put in motion something that he wished he hadn't, so when the meal was pretty well over and he saw Cochrane heading back to his room he got up and followed him.

"I'm sorry," he said, catching up with him just as he was opening the door. "I know you asked us to get out of your way over the Colonel Hetty business, but as it was some comments of mine that set the whole thing off, I feel sort of responsible for her."

"Oh?" Cochrane raised an eyebrow.

"Where is she now? Is she OK?"

"If she isn't," said Cochrane, "it's nothing I've done. Yet."

"No, no. But …" The doctor cast surreptitious glances up and down the corridor. It was carpeted in red, lined with military pictures and free of potential eavesdroppers. "Look, you're obviously going softly, softly," he went on, "and I don't want to teach my grandmother to suck eggs, but the goal isn't just to get her into bed, you know. She has to enjoy it."

Cochrane looked steadily at him saying nothing, and suddenly the doctor started to feel awkward. This sort of talk had never been his medical bailiwick but it wasn't just that. "As you pointed out," he hurried on, "she's forty-some years old and I think there's an outside chance - I don't know how outside - that she's never done this sort of thing before. The word on the street is that if she has a past, it's well past. And even a forty-year-old body isn't twenty.

It isn't even thirty and it won't react as, er, fluidly. Do you know what I'm saying to you?"

"You're saying, or rather trying to say, three things," said Cochrane. "Foreplay, clitoris and lubrication."

The doctor's youth had been post-sexual revolution and he certainly hadn't wasted it, but he didn't remember ever having been this cool a customer. Was it the veterinary education that had done it? Those endlessly long rubber gloves and all the artificial vaginas and electro-ejaculators?

"Well, yes," he said. "I suppose that pretty well sums it up." And he looked again at this handsome twenty-seven-year-old, in whose direct eyes there burned the three-part flame of youth, strength and total confidence, and he wondered where his own had gone. Drained away from him, he supposed, while he'd been trying to do the right thing. And he still didn't know what it was. And if he hadn't had a lovely wife waiting outside for him with a lot of stuff he needed to hear about how he'd dragged her to this lunch and then abandoned her, he'd have gone straight into the bar and got seriously drunk.

He was just retracing his steps when he suddenly turned back and said, "Would it upset you to shoot monkeys in the head, Christopher? Even if you knew it would help someone, not you anymore, but *someone* to save people's lives? Not just soldiers' lives, you understand …"

"It would upset the hell out of me," said Christopher Cochrane, "and every time I looked into their eyes I'd think, 'What gives me the right?' And then I'd reach for the gun and do it. I don't really know what sort of person that makes me."

"No," said the doctor quietly. "That's the problem I have." Setting back off down the corridor, he stopped and turned yet again. "And the Colonel Hetty business?"

"Well," said Cochrane, "that probably makes us look marginally worse. But …," and here he gave an outrageous grin, "I doubt that I'll have to shoot her to get the job done. She may shoot me, of course."

*****

He was still alive a week later when the QM began to express dissatisfaction at having been forced out of the loop. How could they possibly know, he asked, if Cochrane was actually doing anything at all now? He might say he'd slept with Colonel Hetty, was sleeping with her … In fact, he might say all sorts of things, but how could they rely on his integrity?

"Especially when we know what our own is like," pointed out Robbie.

The QM didn't get this but he did get that he might be separated from some carefully hoarded and hidden equipment under false pretences. "I mean, all that talk of two hours," he said. "I bet that was just a load of brag."

"Well, he's laid back all right," said Robbie, considering. "But to be fair, he's never looked like a bragger."

The QM made an impatient noise and turned to the adjutant. "You're about the same age as Cochrane," he said, "and as good-looking. Have you ever met a bird and asked her to have sex within two hours without her looking at you as if you'd just tried to piss in her handbag?"

"No, I haven't," admitted the adjutant, in whom all this talk of two hours was beginning to stir up another bad feeling. A couple of weeks previously, he'd gone to a big media party with his fiancée, where they'd known virtually nobody except the people giving it. Nevertheless, he'd managed to lose her for a good two hours, after which time she'd reappeared, slightly breathless and looking much pinker and prettier, and said that she wanted to go home because she was exhausted and had had enough. In his usual unstirred and unshaken way he'd merely expressed sympathy and gone to fetch her coat.

"No," he repeated. "I've never accomplished anything in two hours from a cold start, but I'm beginning to get a feeling that it happens more often than you'd think."

But the QM wasn't convinced. He'd already forsaken his sacred duty as a quartermaster to give out as little as was humanly possible, and now he might be getting diddled on top of it.

"It's not your equipment anyway," said Robbie irritably. "Though I hate to admit it, if anyone has a say over the fate of this stuff it's now that foul man Henry Pusey, the head of the audit team. I expect he'd like to auction it all off."

"Auction my stores?" exploded the QM. "Henry Pusey? I'd die before I'd let him get his hands on them."

"You may well be called upon to do that," replied Robbie. "And if you are, 1 hope you'll have the strength of character to keep our names out of it."

An unsettled silence followed this. It was the doctor who finally broke it.

Tactfully ignoring all this loose talk of equipment, he said, "I shouldn't worry about not having information direct from Christopher Cochrane. Colonel Hetty will tell you."

Lt Col Mac wasn't normally in the vicinity of HQ at eleven o'clock in the morning - he had his coffee in a bunker somewhere - but today he had come to pick up forms, of which there was now a huge and varied selection to be filled in for everything except bowel movements. Unless you were Sergeant Hoskins, in which case you had forms for that as well. Robbie had finally persuaded him to plead stress of work and try another approach. The details he had to divulge about his health were now intimate and copious and he intended, he said, to blame it all on nerve gas and go for serious compensation.

"You think Colonel Hetty will tell us?" Robbie asked in surprise. "I can just imagine that: 'Oh here, Major Ellis, I want you to charge one hundred pounds per week ground rent for that children's swing set on the rough patch by the quarters. Divide it up amongst the mothers, you know, and bill them monthly on the official notepaper with the swastika in the top corner and, by the way, I'm having very satisfactory sex with Captain Cochrane.'"

"I think that's exactly what she could say," replied the adjutant.

"Well." Lt Col Mac shook his head. "You both know her better than I do, but you obviously realise that if she comes out with two things like that in the same breath, then the whole exercise has been a waste of time. However, I didn't mean that she would actually put it into words for you. Body language, I meant. When Christopher Cochrane is around she'll be larger than life, talk more animatedly, laugh a bit louder."

"All things I would have said were impossible," pointed out the adjutant. "She'll start to look prettier," went on the doctor, ignoring him. "A bit more made up. Her bun might start being less severe, she could develop tendrils …"

"Tendrils aren't allowed," said Robbie.

"What the hell are tendrils?" asked the QM. "What's the man talking about?"

"Honestly," said Mac, looking at them in bewildered impatience, "I don't know how you three get about as regards women."

"Well," said Robbie grimly, "I think it's becoming pretty obvious that we don't."

He'd read the book and seen the movie and he was still in the dark. Women could be courted and made love to, escorted to the altar and delivered of one's children, but they could never, *ever* be assimilated. And after pushing twenty years they couldn't, apparently, be made love to anymore.

"My fiancée's getting prettier," the adjutant whispered to him, "and it's got bugger all to do with me."

Robbie glanced at him in silent sympathy and they both stared thoughtfully out of the window while the QM looked round vacantly. The doctor put his coffee cup down and quietly left.

"Right then," said Robbie presently. "Tendril duty, men. Get to it."

The QM bumped into the chief clerk halfway across the parade square.

"Here," he said, "you put yourself about a bit. Tell me what tendrils are."

"Sir?" The chief clerk looked flummoxed.

"Tendrils," repeated the QM impatiently. "Come on, lad, hurry up. The CO could be about to grow some."

*****

Robbie had to spy on Colonel Hetty in order to get a baseline for hair from which to assess changes. Previously, if pressed, he would have said, after much wrinkling of brows, that Colonel Hetty's hair was short, mousy and masculine, with side-whiskers. Now he saw that it was a rich dark brown and swept back into this bun arrangement that the doctor had mentioned. The side-whiskers were obviously something he had imagined - along with the small Hitler moustache.

Of course, Robbie was also beginning to realise that he wasn't good at this sort of thing. Thinking now about his wife's hair, he visualised it as it had been on their first date, whereas common sense told him that it must have gone through several incarnations since then. None of which he had registered. Had this been a serious omission, he wondered? Along with almost twenty years of his wife doing a twirl in the kitchen and saying, "Well, Robbie?" and him saying, "Well, Robbie, what?" Did that sort of thing matter? Because it hadn't been to do with lack of interest. In fact, he'd recently read in a magazine left in the mess that men were genetically incapable of recognising changes in furniture, clothing or décor of any sort, including hair. Biologically, they were only programmed to detect armed men in the garden and ones with a lot of white teeth who looked likely to make inroads into their bank balances or their wives. Also, and this included the ones with the extra teeth, men had meagre vocabularies compared to women and used them less. A conclusion he'd lately been working towards on his own.

*****

Another week passed, then one day Robbie was passing the CO's office on the way to the adjutant's and as her door was open he glanced inside. Colonel Hetty was lying back in her chair staring unseeingly into space. There was a slight smile playing around her lips and as he watched she seemed to pulse softly and secretly. Then suddenly she came to, stretched languorously like a huge cat, ran her hands down over her breasts, picked up her pen and started work.

Two hours later she called him in. "I took the dogs for a walk last night," she said, in her usual lack-of-preamble way, "and I passed those little paddocks where the children's ponies were kept, and I saw Corporal Brown and his wife picking up droppings, pulling ragwort and hacking down rank grass in preparation for getting a new pony now that Brown's got a promotion. We had quite a nice chat, in fact. It appears, and I'm disappointed that you never mentioned this to me, Robbie, that all of the maintenance is done by the men and their families. Plus, they did the fencing at their own expense. Frankly, I think that the rent on those paddocks should be pretty nominal. I wish this had been made clear to me at the start."

Robbie looked at her and opened his mouth to protest that he had told her all of these things ad infinitum, ad nauseam and then he thought, *She called me Robbie.*

"I'm sorry, ma'am," he said, noticing suddenly that she did indeed have side-whiskers.

"Tendrils," he said quietly to himself.

"Excuse me?"

"Sorry, ma'am. I was thinking of something else."

"Well think about this, Robbie, for heaven's sake. Now, fifty pence per week per pony. How does that sound?"

Of course it didn't all work out like that. The golf range didn't get much cheaper and some idiot went and caught a trout in the Bolney, but the young airman got a last-minute reprieve.

"I decided to just give him a talking-to," said Colonel Hetty.

And Robbie wondered why it all didn't make him feel so much happier.

*****

"Christ!" said the QM one lunchtime. "She looks shagged out."

"I think the word you're looking for is fulfilled," said the doctor. "Beautiful, isn't it?"

"Well, I wouldn't go quite that far," said the QM, who'd never seen a woman fulfilled before, and wasn't really sure he went for it as exemplified by his commanding officer splayed out in a mess armchair.

"Perhaps Cochrane's a tantric sex expert," suggested the adjutant.

"Tantric sex?" asked Robbie. "What the hell's that?"

"I don't know," sighed the adjutant sadly, "but I'm here to tell you that my fiancée has just left me for a man who does."

"Tantric sex," mused Lt Col Mac. "I must get on to that if I'm not too old. Something to do with mysticism, isn't it?"

"Well we're all pretty mystified," said Robbie. "The QM's always been mystified, Jack's mystified about his fiancée, and I'm mystified as to how I can't get my own wife to give me the time of day sexually speaking, and this Christopher Cochrane, with his over-long hair and his American-style salutes, can walk in here and get a semi-lesbian, middle-aged battle axe into a state of glazed acquiescence within a month."

"Well, it's always that way, isn't it?" said Lt Col Mac soothingly. "At first it's all about sex and then, as time passes …"

"It was never that way," said Robbie bitterly. He'd been thinking hard about this and it was coming to him now that he'd never really cut the mustard. He'd always been less than compelling. And now, having dragged his family to Bolney and missed twenty years' worth of hairdos (his wife hadn't been impressed with the genetic explanation of his oversights), he was so far behind on points that he would never catch up. He had no hidden sexual armoury. None of that Hollywood antihero stuff that so bemused Jack. No "I've just come out of the jungle, half-shaved, half-tamed but wholly ready" repertoire to make the hairs on the back of a woman's neck stand up. He was just a decent, hardworking man. And it wasn't enough. And if his wife ever found out about the Colonel Hetty business there would be some serious dispute about whether or not he was even decent.

"Look," the doctor handed them each a whisky, "this was all meant to make us feel better. And Airman James is positively ecstatic, so don't turn it into a dick-measuring contest. It wasn't meant to highlight our own little inadequacies."

"Well my inadequacies are very small," said the QM. "That's why I started going to Thailand."

*****

Christopher Cochrane got his equipment in full measure, although he never gave the frustrated quartermaster any details. The affair was conducted in amazing secrecy for an army camp, and Cochrane behaved like the gentleman that they were all convinced he really wasn't.

When the six months were up, Robbie watched him go with mixed feelings. He didn't want the CO to have some sort of emotional upheaval that would get him right back on the shit list but, at another level, he was glad not to have to keep meeting Cochrane and wondering helplessly, *What has this guy got? What does he do?* Because he felt that one day, he'd make a complete ass of himself by actually asking.

That Colonel Hetty had been changed by her affair with Cochrane was indisputable, but a few weeks after his passing a strange anomaly appeared in her behaviour. She kept her secret little smiles and her air of contentment, but her feelings no longer extended beyond herself. She stopped being relaxed with Robbie and the adjutant, and she began to tighten up on the leniencies that she'd previously instituted. She went away nearly every weekend and visited the mess less in between times.

"You know, Major," she said thoughtfully, just after one of her weekend trips, "I've been thinking that given the scientific work that goes on apace here, we must have a lot of surplus or outdated equipment building up somewhere." Robbie's heart did a huge somersault, landed awkwardly and couldn't function properly for several seconds.

"Equipment?" he squeaked.

"Equipment," he repeated, several octaves lower.

"Yes, you know," said Colonel Hetty, "anaesthetic machines, X-ray machines, that sort of thing."

"I wouldn't know." Robbie strove to look nonchalant.

"Well find out, then."

"She knows," he hissed in the adjutant's ear, grabbing him and propelling him across the square to the QM stores.

"She knows," he said to the QM. "She's on to us."

"It must have been Cochrane, the bastard," said the QM.

"Surely not." The adjutant was less flustered than the other two and thinking more clearly. "I mean, how could he have told her without giving himself away? And why would he? He didn't seem a vindictive chap. Fast," he added reflectively, "and obviously efficient, but not vindictive."

"How else could she know?" asked Robbie.

"The doctor," said the QM. "That smartarse doctor. I bet he told her. We should never have talked in front of him."

"*You* should never have talked in front of him," corrected the adjutant.

"No," said Lt Col Mac. "Never. It wasn't me. *Absolutely not.* You must look elsewhere. But it's interesting, isn't it? Why her behaviour is now so strangely dichotomous." ·

But the other three were too busy envisaging their interviews with the Special Investigations Branch to give his ruminations much attention.

"We'll deny everything," said the QM, who was recovering himself slightly. "It's me that cooks the books round here, not her."

"I doubt you can hide the equipment that's left," said Robbie. "She won't be stopped once she's got the scent of something."

"She's got the scent of nothing that need worry us," said the adjutant. "This is nothing but a clear-out. She can have no idea what was there in the first place."

And that was the way it seemed. A huge unmarked lorry came and emptied the bunkers and the QM got drunk.

"What's giving her these ideas?" he asked dully.

"Search me," said Robbie, taking the bottle of whisky away from him, "but while you're a bit numbed I'm going to forewarn you about a new one she's just had. She's going to civilianise your job."

"Oh, fuck," said the QM. "Let her do it. It's no fun now, anyway."

Which was pretty much how the whole camp felt.

*****

"You know," said Robbie to the adjutant a couple of weeks later. "I think we're actually worse off than we were. I am, anyway. At least before, I could take some spiteful solace from the fact that she was alone and unfulfilled, as the doctor likes to put it. Now, some days she looks as if she's been brought to orgasm by half the cast of *Gladiators* and we ... now we ..." He stopped.

"Are aware of the fact that we've never made a woman look like that?" suggested the adjutant, quietly.

"I was going to say that *we* are now alone, yet still being fucked over." Robbie sighed. "But yes. You're right."

"Has she gone?" the adjutant asked, sympathetically. "Your wife."

"Last week."

"Will she come back, do you think?"

"I don't know. I tried to persuade her to stay. Tried the best I could."

"I don't think I did," said the adjutant. "Looking back, you know."

"Well here's the substitution bill." And Robbie passed across the itemised account for the keep of the polo pony that the adjutant had recently brought up from home.

"Ah, well," Jack got out his cheque book. "Might as well keep in practise for the only type of stick and balling I seem to be any good at."

*****

After a couple of months, when the news that his wife wanted a divorce came through, Robbie packed up his quarter and moved into the mess. He was in the dining room having breakfast one morning when the adjutant came and sat beside him.

"I went to London over the weekend," Jack said. "To see if the tantric sex guy had imploded with the effort."

"And had he?" asked Robbie.

"Sadly, no. Apparently, that almost never happens. However, I found out something that increased my desire to strap myself across the mouth of that new anti-tank gun to an almost irresistible level."

"Oh?" Robbie put down his fork. He still wasn't accustomed to the new emotional Jack.

"I saw the CO in Piccadilly."

"*Really?*"

"With her new lover."

"Do we know him?"

"I'm afraid we do."

"Don't tell me it's Sergeant Hoskins living a new life as a gigolo after his medical discharge."

"You wish," said the adjutant.

"Who, then?"

"Are you sure you're ready for this? Hands away from the cutlery."

"That good, eh?"

"It's Henry Pusey, the chief auditor."

Robbie made a strange noise in his throat and his lips moved but no sound came out.

"I guess that about sums it up," said the adjutant. "We got Colonel Hetty screwed and now it's our turn."

THE FASTIDIOUSNESS OF
FIONA FREDERICKS

Fiona Fredericks was the youngest of eight children. She was also the only girl. Her father, an enthusiastic purveyor of locker-room masculinity, was delighted with the way the sex chromosomes had fallen. He had an income that covered the endless expense and a wife who was happy to rear up a great troop of prop forwards. And the girl, he was fond of saying, was really just to prove that they could do it if they wanted. Besides which, she would be a great help to her mother.

Fiona, of course, didn't want to be a great help to her mother - a handmaiden to half a rugby team. And when puberty hit, the boys' in rapid succession followed by hers, she wanted to do it even less. Nothing that she'd experienced of the male of the species had predisposed her in its favour. It was shameless, godless and in a hurry. It had no concept of hygiene or personal space and it was prurient. Her adolescence was one long embarrassing exposé of her private rites of passage. Her brothers, on the other hand, were unembarrassable - ploughing sweaty, testosterone-driven furrows to adulthood without hitting any sensitive spots whatsoever.

Fiona took baths in bathrooms strewn with discarded underpants, socks and jockstraps. Searched for mugs in a kitchen where everybody else appeared to drink out of milk bottles, juice cartons and beer cans. Found plates while her brothers forked up food from baked bean tins, fish and chip wrappers and takeaway curry cartons. She couldn't sit on the toilet - not even the gardener's outside loo - without somebody leaning against the door and starting up a queue. For, not content with their own numbers, her brothers brought home endless friends who sprawled on the sofas overnight and fetched up scratching and stretching on the landings when she was trying to get into the bathroom on a morning.

"Do I know you?" Getting frosty when hands grabbed the doorknob ahead of her.

"Not yet, but if you'd just let me have a piss, sweetheart, I'll be seriously ready to do something about that." A furious retreat back to her bedroom followed by the thunderous, uninhibited roar of gallons of recycled beer hitting the pan from a great height.

The friends, had Fiona not seen them at their worst, might have been a convenient source of romance for her. Her brothers, having honed her defence mechanisms to a lethal point, saw no reason to be overprotective. In fact, they were not above promoting the odd liaison - pressing a friend's suit in the most appealing way they knew how:

"You know, Jock's a seriously good bloke."

"Not interested."

"Why not?"

"I've overheard some of your conversations with Jock and, on the strength of those alone, I would cross the street to avoid him."

"What conversations?"

"Well specifically, the recurring one where you discuss in detail what you'd like to do to Susie Smythe. Which, incidentally, rather raises the question as to why he isn't asking *her* out?"

"Oh, come on, she's way out of his league."

"And I'm not?"

Fiona chose to overlook the charmless guffaws that followed this. She had a couple of years in which to catch up Susie Smythe in the looks and sex appeal department, though when she finally did it was only distant relatives and strangers who appeared to notice.

"Ma," she said, when she was eighteen years old, "I'm going to this university because there is still a girls' hall of residence, and I'm going to live there in the hope that everyone on my corridor will be either gay or ugly so men won't ever be visiting. I'm doing a course where aforesaid men are likely to be in the minority and after that I'm going to teach in a girls' boarding school."

"My dear child," said her ma. "Do you think you're a lesbian?"

"No," replied Fiona grimly. "But if I pray and I'm patient, maybe it'll come to me."

It didn't, so she still hadn't had even a first kiss when, after university and a PGCE, she applied for a position at a girls' prep school and was subsequently taken on to teach French and hand little girls back to their mamas at five thirty or, alternatively, supervise light-boiled eggs for tea followed by homework and bed. The school had the little girls from seven years old until thirteen and they started out cute and grew to be pretty awful with a penchant for sulkiness and sobbing but, by and large, they didn't have all-over body hair or hammertoes or a fondness for sitting on the loo forever, though it was hell to get them away from the mirrors. Her parents and her brothers (some of whom had persuaded quite intelligent women to hook up with them) visited in dribs and drabs and said, "How can you stand being surrounded by all these girls? Their feet might not be dirty but *boy* can they shriek."

"I don't mind," said Fiona, "and we have a senior school, you know, older girls, up the road. I'm moving there to teach GCSE level next term, which will be nice. They may shriek less."

"As if," said her brothers. "And they'll be heavily into the Malibu."

"Well," Fiona smiled thinly, "they may smuggle in a bit of booze now and then but I have yet to hear of one so shit-faced that she's been found crawling around on all fours with what looks like the tail of a small rodent hanging out of her mouth."

"This one?" asked a future sister-in-law, gazing up fondly.

"Yes," replied Fiona, heavily. "What a rascal."

Where did her brothers find these women? And beautiful. It amazed her.

*****

By the time she was twenty-nine Fiona was expected to be at the school for the rest of her life. "She'll never get married, or even live with anyone," said the other teachers, "attractive as she is. No man will ever be perfect enough for her."

And this was true. Yet, it was also hard. If one wishes to satisfy the desires of nature, then one must be strong enough to ignore the facts of nature. Hard to be heterosexual and not like men.

Fiona did, however, like houses. This came upon her gradually as she passed time looking in estate agents' windows during her trips to town. She was, like Evelyn Waugh's Grimes, "unconsciously pregnant with a desirable villa residence." Undoubtedly, it would be nice to have a home and not just a room above the sanatorium. So when she saw the small cottage within a short drive of the school, she just had to view it. And when she walked through the low front door and realised that her brothers would never be able to visit without bumping their heads, she just had to buy.

She moved in during July, after the end of term, and by the middle of August she was ready to sublimate any nascent sexual urges with some heavy digging. The cottage had once been the gardener's accommodation for a rather grand house which loomed in mysterious stillness beyond an overgrown laurel hedge. Pulling bindweed from under the hedge's canopy and peering through its bare, woody legs, Fiona saw no neighbours but became very familiar with an old Volvo estate car. She never saw it go anywhere, but it did change position on the forecourt now and then. Her compulsion to spy on it became as persistent as the bindweed, so one evening when the sky was turning pink and her back was crying out for a rest, she walked to the bottom of the garden, climbed over the fence into a field and continued to walk the bounds of the big house. On agricultural land the hedge changed from laurel to blackthorn, which was less accommodating of nosy parkers but Fiona managed, as only a dedicated schoolmistress in charge of a mass of giggling adolescent girls knows how, to see what she wanted to see.

The house had a long rear terrace with steps down to sweeping, neglected lawns like small hay fields. Fiona had only a limited view of these, and she spied on them with tunnel vision wherever the gaps in the blackthorn lined up with gaps in the garden's shrubbery.

She'd almost exhausted the speculative possibilities of long grass when she saw him. Emerging from French windows, pushing something stone-coloured that was strapped to a sack truck. He left the sack truck and its load, descended the steps onto the lawn and began to walk around the grounds looking this way and that, pausing and thinking. Into the shrubberies - Fiona drew back. Out of the shrubberies - Fiona crept forward. He came and went in her line of sight with a disconcerting stroboscopic effect until he became all that she could see. Walking in Byronic beauty in the sun, he filled her vision.

He wore baggy khaki shorts and a faded blue shirt that was hanging open to expose a smooth chest and the occasional and totally unexpected wonder of his ribcage. His legs, long and lightly muscled, were thrust sockless into leather hiking boots that he hadn't bothered to lace up. His fingers, when he ran them over the bark of a tree or twirled them thoughtfully round a stalk of grass, were bruised and calloused in places but obviously sensitive. His jawline was clean, his nose straight and his hair a disordered mass of gold. Otherwise, he seemed to have a gratifying absence of hair, an almost girlish beauty. Everything that Fiona found repugnant in men seemed to be tempered or transformed in this young Apollo.

Not too young, of course, she thought hastily. Definitely around thirty. Her heart hadn't beaten this furiously since Sophie Taylor's mother had failed to turn up for the mothers' race and Fiona had felt obliged to pound along in her place. Even then, she hadn't been this breathless. Nothing, *nothing* had prepared her for this huge sucking hole in her chest. This painful, thrilling absence of air. Yet to her credit, she acted like any other red-blooded woman would have done in the circumstances. She ran back to the cottage and looked in the mirror.

Apart from being conscious of the fact that they enabled her to hold her head up amongst her brother's girlfriends, Fiona had never been suitably grateful for her

God-given looks. She had certainly never tried to improve upon them. Teenage attempts at embellishment had been met with discouraging hoots of derision. And she was now aware that she carried more weight with her pupils' mothers when she veered rather the other way. Her beautiful chestnut hair was dragged back, coiled into a rope, twisted into a bun and nailed to her head with hairpins. Certainly it could do with being swept rather than dragged, she thought. And maybe a little softer around her forehead. And then there were eyes to consider - their greenish hue was more than acceptable - but then there was mascara … And lip stuff. God, it was a minefield that she'd done no more than absently register in the bulging bags of girls preparing for an exeat.

She'd resolutely closed her ears to her brothers' full and frank expositions on the subject of female sex appeal. Which seemed to hinge around how many times you had to take a girl to a bistro before you could get into her pants. The fewer the better, apparently. Of course, they'd been young then. And so had she. But now she was a woman and the person she wanted to attract was a man. Full grown. Or possibly a god.

*****

Even with sex appeal reviewed and hopefully established, the problem with having a god on the other side of a twenty-foot laurel hedge was how to bump into him. Especially as she was on a schedule roughly the same as the rest of the mortals on earth, and he was apparently operating on a different part of the space-time continuum. A man who didn't go to work, or wash his car, or garden, or jog, or take a dog for a walk or go to the supermarket. Or come home late on a Saturday night in an impressionable and vulnerable state. A man she could only glimpse in all his glabrous beauty when it was time for another sculpture to be transported onto the lawn. And these times were not predictable. In the following six or seven months, though the sculptures multiplied in number, Fiona saw him only three times. But it was enough.

And then he had an exhibition. At home, on the lawns, with early strawberries and champagne and people in Maseratis and Mercedes and the odd Rolls-Royce. And when you drive an old Mini, thought Fiona, it's probably not the time to try and impress. Still, it was a window of opportunity through which she had to force herself or wait endlessly for another chance, by which time Aphrodite might have moved into the house on the other side and decided to invest heavily in three-dimensional art.

Of course, Fiona still couldn't be sure that there wasn't an Aphrodite already in the picture.

Her brothers, had they known anything about Greek mythology, would have pointed out to her that Apollo arguably conducted the first man-on-man relationship in history. Even without such an intellectual lead in - and she had suffered greatly for being foolish enough to refer to her neighbour as Apollo in the first place - they were wholly confident that a man who smoothed stone and welded metal into faintly suggestive shapes had to be an enthusiastic proponent of Hellenic R and R. A pansy, as her father so indelicately put it. Hugely effeminate, at the very least. But Fiona had cleaned a bathroom after it had been used by most of the London Welsh rugby team, so she took a lenient view of the word effeminate, however un-PC it had become.

A surprising number of the sculptures had red dots on them - especially the ones where she wasn't quite sure what it was a sculpture of, but just wanted to keep looking whilst running a hand over its cool, smooth curves.

"Excuse me, but you're my next-door neighbour, aren't you?"

A miracle. Not only had he registered her presence, but somehow he knew who she was. A godlike ability to see over a twenty-foot hedge from deep within the bowels of the house whilst blinded by marble dust and an arc welder.

To see her crouched in the blackthorn? Peering under the laurel?

"Oh God!" said Fiona. She'd come bravely up the drive, been presented with a stiff and impressive information leaflet, the prices on which had left her numb with shock, and she was now busy slinking back home through the shrubbery. No wonder he'd recognised her.

"Luke will do," he said with a golden smile, holding out a hand.

"I wasn't invited," said Fiona. "I was just being nosy. The prices are a little out of my league, I'm afraid." *Well done, girl*, she added silently, *that should be crass enough*.

"Out of my league too," said Luke with a glance at the

house roof which was now half-covered in tarpaulins and stacks of tiles.

"You're doing that yourself?" Fiona had seen no sign of builders.

"With my own hands. Unfortunately, it's taking forever as I have just the one pair."

"You should have been a Hindu god instead of a Greek one."

"Excuse me?"

"Nothing." But what hands they were. Suffering, as she'd previously noticed, for their dedication to art but no gnawed fingernails and no rings.

"Don't run away," said Luke. "Especially not through the vegetation. Come and have a drink. Should we take the leaves from your hair first?"

Fiona put up her hands in horror. It had taken two hours to achieve a look that smacked of not having tried at all, and now it had acquired a discomforting authenticity.

"You could tidy up in the bathroom," suggested Luke. "The one just at the top of the main staircase still has running water. But here, let's get the goose grass off your back first."

"It all looks like an impromptu romp in the bushes to me," remarked a stunning girl who commandeered Luke as soon as Fiona shot off. "Who on earth is she? I hope she brought a cheque book."

"She's my next-door neighbour."

"How very suburban."

There was no queue. People who pay thousands of

pounds for sculptures don't go to the toilet. Their internal plumbing, like everything else about them, is infinitely superior to everyone else's. She splashed her red face, removed twigs and clips from her hair and shook it out. But mostly, she looked at the bathroom. No whiskers in the basin, no rugger rings round the bath, no ball of body hair in the plughole, no unpleasant stickiness on the tiles round the toilet bowl. He could have a very efficient cleaner. Or, he could be gloriously and wonderfully different.

Back on the lawn, she sipped champagne and drank in sculptures. She was among the beautiful and the informed so naturally she was destined to drink alone. Nobody acknowledged her, though the talk was animated and authoritative enough for her to hear. Luke was obviously in great demand, and when she finally began to feel that she could no longer make solo studies of his work without looking ridiculous, she decided to find him, express appreciation, and leave. Having decided to do this, she needed half an hour's mental rehearsal before she could get her legs to move in his direction. Then she had to lurk hideously, waiting for a gap in the conversations he was having with people who were much more adept at getting his attention than she was. Catching his eye at last, she was able to produce a well-rehearsed and passably sophisticated effort at expressing how much pleasure his work had given her.

He was charming, of course. Delighted, he said. "I'll see you again," he added as she turned to walk away.

I doubt it, she thought. All around her people were gradually drifting back to their cars calling, "We must do lunch sometime," in voices ringing with insincerity.

"Who was that?" a man asked Luke.

"My next-door neighbour."

"Amazing looks. Like a girl out of a Burne-Jones painting."

"Yes," said Luke. "That's what I thought."

*****

For the next three weeks, Fiona had an uncharacteristic sympathy with the fourth-formers sobbing over boy bands. There was a churning in her chest. She woke during the night with this feeling, arose with it and took it back to bed with her. How long before it wore off?

It was a month to the day after the exhibition, a Saturday morning, when she answered a knock to find Luke on the doorstep. He was holding out a bunch of wine-coloured roses, evidently picked from his garden.

"Oh, such a smell," said Fiona. "Madame Isaac Perrier."

"No idea," confessed Luke. "It's the only one that seems to withstand all the neglect I heap upon it."

The transferring of the posy was difficult because of the thorns. After several oohs and ouches, Luke said: "It seems rather crass to ask someone as lovely as you out on a date at such short notice, but would you be free tonight?"

Fiona was speechless. The grace, the fluency, the guileless charm of the invitation. The contrast with her experience of Jock, for instance, who'd been "such a seriously good bloke."

"Of course, if you're married or something," he added hastily into the silence, "it's considerably more than crass."

"I'm not married," said Fiona. "Not anything. I'll come. Coffee?"

"Sorry," said Luke. "I'm waiting for something to set." And he disappeared.

So Fiona didn't know what time she was going, where she was going, or what she was going to do when she got there. Superfluous to add that she didn't know what to wear.

It was her first date. Ever. She'd always known too much about men to want to date one. Now, she found the tension unbearable. All her fantasies seemed ludicrous. Worse than ludicrous. Insane. This man, beautiful as he looked, couldn't possibly be that much different. He seemed to live alone. Supposing he ate like he'd just had to go out and catch the stuff and blood ran down his chin. He was a man, for God's sake - too leaky a vessel to hold so much hope.

She got ready for five thirty and sat stiffly like a portrait of Queen Victoria (and in a comparable sort of dress) till Luke turned up at seven forty-five.

"What time did I say?" were his first words, hastily followed by, "Oh God, I didn't, did I?"

"It's fine," said Fiona. "This is a fine time."

"What a relief." Luke gave a sigh. "I'm vague on time. I work when I feel like it, eat when I feel like it, and sleep when I feel like it. No real grasp of the twenty-four-hour clock."

"Well, the muse is reputedly fickle," said Fiona.

"Exactly," said Luke. "That's exactly right. I can see we're going to get along."

He was easy to talk to and easy to sit in silence with. As they walked home, afterwards - a pleasant undulating mile - he picked up her hand and held it carefully, swinging her arm backwards and forwards as if they were just six years old. They talked about the full moon and the briar roses hanging pale and luminous in the hedgerows, and what she had planned for her garden and what hopes he had for a big commission he'd received. And how it had been a nice idea to walk to the local pub but terrible to have to eat the food, especially for Luke who was vegetarian. "No great crusade," he said. "I just don't like eating corpses."

*****

"Definitely gay," said her brothers - a hard core of whom still regularly turned up at home for Sunday lunch.

"Why did I tell you this?" said Fiona. "Why would I do that? Oh, that's right, I didn't. Ma did. When is she going to learn to keep secrets like other people's mothers have to do?"

"Fiona," said her mother, "I worry about you. You're nearly thirty years old, the biological clock is ticking and now, somewhat out of the blue, you've fallen for a man who hasn't even kissed you on the cheek after two dates. I needed a second opinion."

"And a third and a fourth and so on ..." said Fiona. "And all of them deeply and nauseatingly predictable. Has it ever occurred to you that he could just be nice? And polite?"

"And gay," finished her brothers.

*****

"He's not gay," Fiona told herself firmly and loudly as she studied her new flower border whilst waiting for Luke to arrive for their fifth date. "I know he's not."

"How do you know?" asked Luke, who had come quietly down the garden path.

"I was assuming that fate couldn't possibly be that unkind."

Luke put his arms round her. "Kiss me."

"I'm sorry," he said quietly, when he finally lifted his head. "I'm slow at this sort of thing. I'm on my own so much, l really don't know how it's supposed to go. I was just busy enjoying your conversation and your company and falling in love with you."

"God," breathed Fiona. And she meant it.

*****

"He's not normal," said her brothers. "He might not be a fully-fledged something or other but he can't be normal living alone in that great house with no sexual outlet other than fiddling with inert substances. Until you come along. It's a classic, isn't it? He's into child pornography and you're the nearest thing to a child that he can take to the pub for a drink."

"And the nearest thing to inert."

"You lot," said Fiona furiously, "are the only people I know who have even a passing acquaintance with pornography."

*****

She and Luke had been going out for six months - a slow and highly pleasurable six months - when they finally went to bed together.

"There's something I must tell you," said Fiona. "I've never done this before."

"What a relief," said Luke. "Neither have I."

"*Never*?"

"No."

How could this possibly be? How could a man this beautiful and civilised not have been taken against his will?

"But all those stunningly confident, rich women at your sculpture exhibition? None of them ever got you into bed?"

"An exhibition is only once every few years," said Luke.

But once was enough. Fiona thought of the determination exhibited by her girls when they had the Christmas dance with the nearby boys' school.

"Sculpture is a passion," said Luke, slowly. "A fire. It can consume all the fuel you have."

"But before you were a serious sculptor?"

"I was shy," said Luke. "And besides, my brothers had enough sex for all of us. I suppose I had it vicariously in the morning-after conversations. Shameful, really."

Fiona knew the feeling. She rarely talked about her own brothers because she knew that what they'd been saying could show in her eyes.

"But what I lack in expertise, I'll make up for in love," he promised.

"Just one question first," said Fiona. "Why me?"

"Promise you won't be cross?"

"Promise."

"You were the only person at my exhibition who looked more embarrassed than I was."

But there all embarrassment ended. Love is not embarrassed and it knows what to do.

*****

"You're going to move into that great barn of a house with him?" Her mother was shocked. "My dear, the roof isn't even on properly and you just got your cottage so pretty and the garden and, and ..."

"And all the things you're going to find hidden in the wardrobes. And the dead mother in the rocking-chair," said her brothers. "And the bloodstains on the shower curtain."

"I'm just grateful he's *got* a shower curtain," said Fiona grimly. "And knows how it works."

"How come he could buy a huge house like that, anyway?" asked her father. "Is the boy monied?"

"He inherited it when his parents died," said Fiona, wearily. "It was the family home."

*****

"And my brothers hated it," explained Luke, one December evening as they stood on its frosty lawns looking at the tarpaulins still on the roof and the cluster of magnificent Gothic chimneys backlit by a silvery winter moon. "I don't think it was anything personal against the poor house. Ever since D of E they just never liked living in houses. Had to be under canvas. And the farther away the better - desert plains, polar ice caps, the decks of banana boats - any place where they didn't have to wash up for tea. But the house is perfect for me because the sound of shearing metal and splintering stone going on twelve hours a day tends to distance you from your neighbours if you aren't distanced already."

"Your brothers," said Fiona, "sound very similar to mine."

"But not me," replied Luke, a shade sadly. "I was always the odd one. Family folklore has it that I'm a throwback to a lover of my grandmother's who was an impoverished artist. I gather that Grandmama married for money and saw what could be done about the artist afterwards."

*****

"I'll make you your own space here," he said, a few days later. "A room, a study, whatever, where you can put your things and escape from Grandmother's mahogany - and me, should the urge ever come upon you. You can have the best view and a bathroom attached for your makeup and all the stuff women like to do with the door shut."

This man *is* a god, thought Fiona in amazement. How else could he understand these things?

*****

"Marry me," he said a couple of months later, when Fiona was admiring the new plumbing he'd done and the size of the bathroom cupboard he'd built.

"Really?"

"Marry me, *please*."

"All right," said Fiona. "I don't think that's too high a price to pay for a bidet."

"We'll do the whole place up," he said, when he'd finished kissing her. "If you can't stand being surrounded by other people's furniture I'll get rid of it. Just as soon as I've explained the situation to my brothers. It's just a politeness, but I'd feel easier if I did it. I have a relatively recent poste restante address for one of them at the bottom of Kilimanjaro or somewhere."

"The furniture's fine," said Fiona. "I don't want to oust the heirlooms of the family that produced the perfect man for me."

"So how soon can we get married?"

*****

"Fiona," said her brothers, "we have serious reservations about this guy. Why doesn't he want you in his bathroom? Have you looked in the cupboards for the amyl nitrite and the hoods?"

"It's not that he doesn't want me in his bathroom," Fiona replied. "He just understands what I need. And without my having to explain."

"He's heading for trouble," said her father. "Giving his wife her own boudoir and lavatory. Bloody silly idea. Next thing he'll be looking for a surrogate mother to bear his children so you don't have to be inconvenienced."

"Now, now," intervened her mother, soothingly. "We all know that Fiona's very fastidious. She would never dream of having her ova transferred into another woman. You'll gestate your own children, won't you, dear?"

"I'll only do it if I can have girls," said Fiona savagely. "I think somebody's found a system for that."

*****

Luke and Fiona were married a month later in a little local church, with Fiona's brothers and father muttering in the aisles, and Luke's letter to his brothers about the furniture, plus their wedding invitations, uncollected at the bottom of Kilimanjaro.

With so much to do to the house it seemed frivolous to have an exotic honeymoon but there was a long weekend in South Devon, walking on windswept beaches, listening to the wild cries of gulls and making love in front of a log fire.

"We could retire here when we're old," said Luke, "and leave the house to the grown-up babies."

"Not eight babies," said Fiona.

*****

Three months later, when the fifth form were doing GCSEs and the seniors doing A levels, Fiona had to accompany fourth form girls on a school trip to Athens. She didn't enjoy it because she didn't want to leave Luke and because she couldn't interest the girls in the restoration of the Parthenon because they were too busy looking for Greek gods. *At least*, she thought, as she rested on dusty steps and pulled back her damp hair, *I know it's possible to find one.*

The return flight came in at nearly midnight, so after helping the other teacher see the girls safely into the school dormitories she drove home, ran upstairs without even a pause to put on the lights, and slid into bed with Luke. He was in one of his deep, post-creative sleeps and, uncharacteristically, still smelt of stone dust and hot metal with a hefty overlay of what Fiona's long-term memory recognised as stale male sweat. His back, when she laid her cheek against it, had a greasiness that was entirely new.

Waking up, he turned over.

"Miss me?" she asked.

"Get on it, sweetheart," he said, "and find out."

He had at least three days' worth of stubble, which provided some entirely new and frankly raw sensations, in addition to which he had put on weight, or muscle, or something that made him feel heavier, stronger and, well, not forceful but certainly more difficult to slide out from under.

"Love you," he murmured, dropping into instant post-coital narcosis.

"Even afterwards?" asked Fiona, poking him.

"Sure."

Fiona stared at the ceiling with the odd feeling that she'd visited the USA and fallen asleep in the Catskills like Rip

Van Winkle instead of having taken a relatively brief trip to Athens.

She should have been exhausted but she couldn't stay asleep for longer than ten minutes at a stretch. She felt unsettled. Guilt, she told herself, for sneaking away from her school duties. She knew that as soon as the girls woke up there would be post-holiday grumpiness and a lost luggage problem to sort out. Gucci suitcases somehow en route to Baghdad.

She got up at dawn without disturbing Luke, weary but restless, thinking that she might just as well get on with the day. But no sooner had she set her bath running and plumped down on the loo than she was gripped by that familiar feeling of someone forming a queue outside. She listened. There was no noise. Just the stirring of a sixth sense honed through years of programming. Or was there a shape? Beyond the etched glass of the Victorian door?

"Luke?" She got up and flushed the toilet, pulling down her nightdress.

"Luke?" She opened the door.

Face-to-face now with a huge hairy stranger dressed only in some sort of disgusting loincloth that might once have been a towel. He was propping himself against the wall with one grubby paw spread out on the pale blue Colefax and Fowler wallpaper at thirty pounds a roll, whilst he attended to some early morning self-grooming that involved picking fluff out of his navel and using one black-rimmed, hairy big toe to scratch the enormous calf muscles of the other leg.

"Do I know you?" Fiona asked coldly.

"Nope." Heavily bearded grin, one front tooth broken. "But you're going to." And he was into the bathroom, *her* bathroom, her *personal* bathroom, before the corner of her nightdress had even vacated it. Then there was a contented low grunt and the sound of gallons of urine hitting the pan. Without even shutting the door properly.

"Hey!" shouted Fiona. "What do you think you're doing in there?"

"What's it sound like?"

"It sounds like you've peed in my loo and are now getting into my bath."

"We'll have to share now there's seven of us."

"*Seven of us!* Would you care to explain?"

"Come and scrub my back, sweetheart, and I'll tell you anything you want to know."

"Luke! *Luke!*" She rushed along the landing noticing, in the increasing light of day, the shadowy heaps of rucksacks and piles of filthy-looking Banana Republic clothing down in the hall. "*Luke, there's a man in my bath!*"

"Yes, darling. Isn't it wonderful?" Luke sat up in bed, looking strangely un-Luke-like. Eyes bloodshot, teeth a flash of white in a heavily stubbled face, muscles rippling under a gleaming film of sweat. "The brothers came back for our wedding. Months late, of course, but they've brought us a marvellous set of blowpipes and a stuffed python. Hell to get through customs, but there's no stopping the boys when they've made their minds up."

"Boys," repeated Fiona weakly. "*Boys?*" She thought of

the fifteen-stone Piltdown man sitting in her bath.

"Yes," said Luke. "And do you know? I never thought I'd be glad to see them home. They gave me hell when I was young, set off all sorts of complexes. Made me feel a bit girly, to tell the truth, with the art and all. But when they saw the wedding pictures of you … Well, all that changed, I can tell you."

"Did it?" Some heavy inflection in there which passed unnoticed.

"They were envious, Fiona. Actually envious of *me*! Can you imagine it? All that tramping round the world, they said, and they hadn't picked up anything as wonderful as I'd found at home. For the first time *ever* I really feel like one of them. One of the boys. And the best thing is that they're going to stay for a while, take a rest from travelling, write up some papers, you know. And help us sort things around the house. I said you'd be delighted. Told them about your seven brothers. A houseful of men will be nothing to Fiona, I said. That's right, isn't it, darling?"

Pain shot through Fiona's heart like cracks through glass. She took in the pile of dirty boxer shorts and socks on the bedroom floor and through welling tears she saw a matt of hair growing over the beautiful smooth chest of her Greek god. And she said sadly, "That's right, Luke. A houseful of men means nothing to me. Absolutely nothing."

THE ORACLE AT THE
ROSE AND CROWN

Bill at the pub wasn't what you would call intellectual - or even particularly bright - but he saw things. He was instinctive. In touch. A couple of centuries ago they might have called him a seer. Or an idiot savant. Certainly, he wasn't inspirational to look at - a man out of whose mouth you didn't necessarily want to hear your future pouring.

An ageing hippie who had hung (barely) onto the ponytail, though not the beads, he still wore the sandals because his feet hurt. Also he'd had four wives, two of them at the same time, which might have led a sceptic to feel that he was lacking in prescience rather than the other way round. Still, the fact remained that he was as prescient as you got in the Rose and Crown. If you liked draught bitter and you wanted an insight, Bill was where you ended up.

One Friday night, working his way across the bar, Joe Gallagher sidled up to him. Sidling was a bad move in the Rose and Crown. Especially in the vicinity of Bill. As one animal, fellow patrons tended to sidle along with you. A comradely wave of sidling, with conversations nipped in the bud and soundless sips at the beer.

Joe crossed Bill's palm with a double whisky and said, "My wife ..." in a furtive whisper that everyone found enormously encouraging because it was bouncing back off the Jack Daniels mirrors at such a fortuitous angle. "... my wife has a ... thingie."

"A thingie?" asked Bill. Even seers need more information than that.

"*You* know," said Joe with a weak gesture that was supposed to demonstrate but petered out because every eye in the bar, including two fox terriers' and one belonging to the landlord's parrot, was trained on it.

"You'll have to be more specific."

Joe took a deep breath. He wasn't a man for sharing confidences about his wife. Or about anything. He was two hundred and fifty pounds of hard-earned inhibitions that you could squeeze with pliers - maybe not forever but for as long as it should interest you - without extracting a whine. He'd been brought up on the principle that least said was soonest mended. And don't complain. Somebody drives over his foot, blood seeps into his sock, out through the lace-holes in his boots: "No, I'm fine. Absolutely fine."

He'd been raised in a place where steelworks were silent and men were more silent still. He knew you had to take what you got. So it was a measure of his great anxiety about the "thingie" that he was prepared to share it with Bill in what could turn out to be less of a private conversation and more of a group therapy session. "A vibrator," he whispered.

"What?" Bill was a bit deaf. Led Zeppelin's fault.

"A vibrator."

"What's a vibrator?" asked the old man with the fox terrier.

"A sex aid," said the youth next to him. "A machine that women touch themselves up with. Electric."

"*Electric?*" The old man's eyes watered. "I had no idea it was so hard to be a woman."

"How big is it?" asked Bill. "Is it bigger … You know?"

"Longer maybe," said Joe, "if you count the handle."

"There's a dangerous attractiveness to these things," said Bill. "I believe they're extremely efficient."

This set off another widespread bout of shuffling as bedside tables were mentally reviewed. Also bathroom cupboards and women's underwear drawers.

"Of course, they can't do everything we can do," said Bill.

"Like cut the lawn," pointed out the barman.

"And just because she uses this thing, it doesn't mean she doesn't love you," added Bill. "I'm sure she does love you."

Joe downed some beer. He wasn't feeling convinced. "But she must think about something while she's doing it. If it's me then what's the point?"

"Maybe you're better in theory," suggested the barman.

"They're just thoughts," said Bill. "Same as we have."

"*Christ!*" exclaimed the youth.

Joe flushed. "Well, we're men," he said. "I thought

women were, well, romantic. Liked to get fanciful about a particular person. We're more, er, practical."

"It must get practical for them too," said the barman, "at some stage in the proceedings, or why would they do it?"

"Look," said Bill. "Often these things are just a matter of convenience. Women of a certain age - your wife's age, Joe, in their late forties, you know - they have rushes."

"Flushes?"

"No, rushes."

Rushes, thought Joe, taking another drink. That might not be all bad. He could stand to be rushed the odd time. In fact, he could do with it. Not rushed as in hurried, but rushed as in "the baddies overpowered the hero by rushing him." Yes, he could enjoy being rushed by Lorraine. Think of all the agonising it would save. The confusion. Is she in the mood? Should I or shouldn't I? What does the embroidered pillow say? Is it turned to the side where it reads: "Don't even think about it!"? Is she busy making a new one with a cross-stitched tombstone in the middle and gothic lettering: "Here lies the last son-of-a-bitch who tried to rush me"? So having Lorraine rush *him* ... Now that would really be something. He finished his pint and ordered a whisky while he allowed this pleasing fantasy to flourish a little.

"Sometimes they don't want sex for ages," said Bill. "And sometimes they want it a lot. Maybe several times a day. It's how their hormones work in middle age."

"So let's get this right," said Joe. "Every so often a big

bolus of oestrogen hits their brains and for about twenty-four hours they're pretty well nymphomaniacs?"

"Yes," said Bill.

"Well I can't say I've noticed that."

A sentiment that was strongly shared up and down the bar.

"You wouldn't, would you?" said Bill. "That's what she has the vibrator for."

"Have some more whisky," said the barman, giving Joe's arm a sympathetic squeeze.

More whisky and more comment from Bill, and Joe still wasn't soothed. Lorraine had to be thinking of somebody during these rushes. He wouldn't have wanted to put a week's wages on betting it was him.

"I can't live with this," he said finally. "I really can't stand the thought of it."

"In that case," said Bill, "there's only one thing to do, one thing that will make this go away."

"What?" asked Joe eagerly. "How? And will it work?"

"It'll work."

An expectant and respectful hush fell over the bar.

"Yes?"

"It's hard," said Bill, "but there's no alternative. You have to sleep with another woman."

"*What?*" Joe almost exploded. Damn right it was going to be hard! It was difficult enough getting to have sex with Lorraine. The thought of trying to get it on with another one … *Jesus*! Plus … "Why would it work?"

"I just get these feelings," said Bill. "This knowledge. I can't always analyse it."

"Try," said Joe.

"Maybe it's just a psychological thing," suggested the barman. "To help you even things up. Level the score, as it were."

"Is that it, Bill?" Joe asked.

"Could be," said Bill.

"How many runs would it take?" asked Joe, anxiously.

Bill stared deep into his glass. "Could be that you'll only have to do this once."

"Once," said the barman. "Come on, Joe, how hard can it be?"

Joe had another pint. He just didn't see an extramarital escapade as an option. Women were like a book in a foreign language to him. Interesting to look at but uninformative. Most of the time, he was struggling to find one sentence that made sense. He'd never get a strange one into bed. Even if he was really trying, which was when he was at his most inept and which he didn't feel much like. Even drunk, which he was rapidly becoming.

"Bill," he said. "Can't you rethink this? Run it again?"

"I've given you my advice," said Bill. "Whether you take it or not is up to you."

The prescience was over.

Joe sat for a while longer, had another whisky then started to feel bad and decided he ought to go home. He left the bar amidst sympathetic pats on the back. Outside, the cold air hit him like a dam bursting and he was just orientating himself when a sultry voice said: "Joe, would you like to come home with me?"

Joe jumped. "What?"

"Would you like to come home with me?"

"What for?"

"Sex."

Joe had waited for an invitation like this for the best part of his youth and it had never come. With his friends losing their virginity left, right and centre, he'd been tongue-tied to the sacrificial rock waiting for the dragon. Thirty years and a rite of passage too late, here she was.

"Do I know you?" he asked.

"I come here now and then," she said. "I know you."

Hmm. Joe wondered if she'd overheard his conversation with Bill. And immediately a vision of the vibrator rose in his head, working rhythmically away like a pile-driver. And about the same size.

"What time is it?" he asked.

"Ten o'clock."

Joe felt fuzzy. Lorraine would still be at that women's book group, wouldn't she? Probably getting a lot of input that a marriage could do without. Meeting a lot of feminists who wanted to be pile-drivers.

"All right," he said, and the woman stepped out of the shadows and took his arm.

"What's your name?" he asked.

"Dora," she said. "Short for Pandora." And she smiled.

*****

Joe got home at two o'clock in the morning and crawled into bed, too addled to think of showering. And too late anyway. He could barely remember what he'd done but some of it had made him go numb from the waist down and forget his own name for a while. He smelt of beer, stuff he ought to have washed off, and some strange perfume like old fruit salad that made him feel nauseous. It was nothing like Lorraine wore. He should have known just looking at that woman that her taste wouldn't be quite on the button. In brighter light she'd looked like someone he'd once played football with.

He woke earlier than he would have liked on account of the steadily increasing weight of the suitcase that was lying on his legs. A new sort of numbness overtook him as he watched Lorraine systematically filling it.

"Where are you going?" he asked, finally.

"To a friend's," she said. "Until you come up with an explanation I'm prepared to accept. It seems unlikely that you will, but when you're sober enough you might want to start working on it."

Joe was just about to do the male equivalent of bursting into tears when he saw that the vibrator was being packed too - lying insolently in pride of place on top of some underwear. He made a violent lunge for it and Lorraine said sharply: "Leave that alone. I want to use it before I go."

"Use it?" Joe said weakly. "With me here?"

"Of course with you here," said Lorraine. "You think I should wait for you to be clear-headed enough to get out the bedroom before I can get on?"

Joe watched, stunned, while she picked the thing up, unscrewed the end, took out two batteries (run low how quickly, he wondered bitterly) and put in two new ones. Then she sat on the end of the bed and held it in her hand for a while. Ran her fingers up and down the shaft just like it was a … Well, Joe was appalled. When she was satisfied, she turned to the dressing table and adjusted the mirrors carefully so that she had a view of herself from all angles. (Joe thought he was going to be sick.) Then she sat down on a stool, felt the vibrator thoroughly one more time, and straightened her hair with it.

THE PHILOSOPHER AND
THE PLUMBER

Isabella Stone was a philosopher. A surprising occupation, perhaps, in the third millennium when science appears to have ousted philosophy to such an extent that the man on the Clapham omnibus could be forgiven for wondering what on earth a philosopher would do all day. Bella thought about time. That was the subject of her latest paper. A spinoff from her doctorate, it was a comparison of the current theories on the means by which human consciousness establishes the temporal order of perceived events.

And when she wasn't thinking about time, Bella was giving tutorials to undergraduates and lecturing them on symbolic logic. It's essentially a cerebral occupation being a philosopher - especially at a university like Cambridge where written output is expected to be exceptional – and it can leave a person less than equal to the task of changing a tap washer. Which is unfortunate, as Bella soon discovered, because the other significant thing about being an up-and-coming philosopher is the level of remuneration. Plumbers are much better paid and, strangely enough, even harder to come by.

These were two salient facts which made Bella wish that she hadn't decided quite so precipitately to move into the brick cottage on the edge of town that had been left to her by her grandfather. A grandfather who hadn't exactly been Rachman, but who had accumulated property in indecent quantities and paid for it by collecting indecent rents at a time when that sort of thing had gone largely unregulated. Nevertheless, Grandfather's egregious prescience in the property business had enabled Bella's mother and father to live very comfortably as artists and authors without actually selling much of their work. And their rather Bloomsbury lifestyle had provided the perfect setting in which a growing child could learn to be especially philosophical - as Bella discovered at ten years of age when she walked in on her mother and a lesbian lover. And it was just as well that she learned quickly, because the lesbian lovers had a high turnover rate and her father had to do what he could to comfort them – which seemed to be quite a lot, and not all of it in the true spirit of lesbianism. So it was a little confusing, even for a born philosopher. Anything seemed to go as long as it was kept at an intellectual, arty and culturally superior level where it became a form of creative self-expression. The parental Stones did not fuck the proletariat – not in the most specific sense of the word. In fact, they had very little contact with the proletariat. And neither did Bella. Until the day she bought a washer dryer.

This washer dryer, a relatively big investment for

someone who was still paying off a student loan, was a sudden and desperate countermeasure to tedious sessions in the laundrette, a dearth of central heating in the cottage and the fact that hand-washed, hand-wrung clothes were prepared to drip in the garden for days, contentedly exchanging water molecules with the damp spring air.

"Where's the plumbing?" asked the delivery man, easing the machine off the trolley and into the small scullery next to Bella's kitchen.

"Plumbing?" Bella looked round vaguely. She understood the word, of course, she just couldn't visualise it.

"Where the clean water goes in and the dirty water comes out," explained the delivery man.

"Right," said Bella. That sort of thing had taken care of itself in the laundrette so she simply hadn't thought about it. Thinking about time doesn't leave much of it over for pondering the mundane. "So how does that happen then? Where do I get plumbing from?"

"From a plumber," said the delivery man. "At a cost roughly equivalent to the price of the machine."

"About three hundred pounds?" Bella was horrified. She'd paid for the washer dryer with money from her mother, but she'd never anticipated a huge surcharge to get the thing to work. "And where do I find a plumber?"

"Google," said the delivery man. And then disappeared - leaving behind a lot of polystyrene that he ought to have taken with him.

*****

"So now I've got the bloody thing and I can't use it," Bella said crossly to her lover that evening. He was forty-five years old, this lover - almost twenty years her senior and the professorial head of the philosophy department. He had rather wonderful grey hair like Richard Gere, rimless glasses and a stunning intellect. So one way and another he didn't fit comfortably into the category of "boyfriend." In any case, Bella was used to the word "lover" because her parents had used it so frequently. Of course, it had that mischievous and misleading word "love" in the middle but Bella wasn't analysing love at the moment, she was preoccupied with time because the regular production of papers which would get published in prestigious journals was the way for her to get onto the tenure track. Consequently, she wasn't getting at all hung up, philosophically or emotionally, on the *love* input to the word lover. But, irritatingly enough, she caught herself devoting a certain amount of her precious time to a consideration of the word "satisfaction."

"No flatmates anymore," said her professor, unbuttoning her shirt and running his hands over her pert, braless breasts. "Much more convenient, isn't it?"

Bella had tried to get him interested in the washer dryer but he wasn't a professor of plumbing after all, although he had speculated – just a shot in the dark here – that maybe the washer dryer could be got to work more cheaply by shoving the red and blue hoses onto the taps of the Belfast sink in the scullery and poking the outlet hose down the plughole. An arrangement that he was not prepared to elaborate upon in any practical way.

"Nice not to be concerned about people barging in," he said.

But not quicker, I hope, thought Bella who occasionally found it irritating that the professor's lovemaking was as fast as his thought processes. He was keeping an eye on her intellectual effort together with the length of her legs, the tightness of her bottom, the luxuriance of her long dark hair and the fullness of her big soft mouth. He supervised all of these things with dedication, but he stopped short at her orgasms. Of these he was oblivious. Well not oblivious, exactly, because that could imply that they happened but he missed them. In fact they didn't happen and he didn't miss them. But such was his grasp of temporal order under normal circumstances that Bella had been overlooking this. Plus, though her professor was capable of advanced and stimulating argument on any amount of subjects, she somehow knew that he would become enormously sulky if his sexual technique was held up for critical analysis.

"Should we go upstairs?" she asked.

"Since no one is going to walk in," he replied, "why don't you just bend over the table?"

People in media productions are forever getting bent over tables or desks or kitchen counters – both forwards and backwards – and apparently having a high old time of it within a matter of moments. But that's on television. Which Bella had little interest in - with the result that she had never been programmed to utilise furniture with anything like the same level of success. Too busy fielding unwashed crockery and half-empty milk cartons and scattered breakfast cereal.

When her professor had finished he zipped up smartly, dropped a quick kiss on her shoulder and hurried away because he had someone else from the department bringing him a paper on ontological emergence. Bella pulled up her jeans with a sigh. Sometimes, she felt that Professor Niall Grayson took an Einsteinian view of sex, i.e., that it simply cleared the mind for thought.

She went back into the scullery and looked from the red and blue hoses of the washer dryer to the taps of the Belfast sink, wondering how these could best be persuaded to have a successful and enduring mating. She knew that there was no point in asking any of the men she knew (especially not her father) for advice on practical matters, so the next day she rode her bicycle to B&Q and talked to a spotty youth with his name on his lapel who kitted her up with some rubber bits and brass bits, some jubilee clips and a pair of mole grips at what seemed an exorbitant price.

She took these home and got them, not without difficulty, out of the transparent shrink wrapping and laid them on top of the washer dryer. How hard could it be? Pretty hard, as it turned out. She had the bits, the wrench, a brain and two hands just like a plumber, but still she ended up soaking wet - as did the scullery floor, walls and ceiling. Reading instructions and following diagrams was one thing, but joining together the pipes and taps that she held in her hands was quite another. They just wouldn't stay joined. It was unbelievable. And such a trivial thing. And philosophers, of course, are not grabbed by trivia. The problems that concern them are of cosmic significance - which was why Bella was always coming home to an empty fridge, a full sink and an unmade bed. These things simply weren't cosmic enough to be dealt with. But trivialities have to be dealt with or civilised life comes to an end, and Bella didn't want to live in a barrel like Diogenes so she went and got her laptop.

The internet wasn't at its fastest and she had to follow up with phone calls so she didn't do an exhaustive investigation into plumbers in the Cambridge area, but she found out enough to reach what seemed like two statistically valid conclusions:

1. Plumbers are not prepared to come out and push rubber hoses onto taps.

2. If one had been, the call-out fee would have been astronomical and she wouldn't have seen him this side of Christmas.

*****

A couple of days later, she was in the back garden hanging out dripping jeans and mentally badmouthing plumbers when she was hit by a blast of exhaust fumes. The neighbours on her left didn't have cars that started up and went away in the morning and came back and switched off in the evening like everybody else's. Their cars just stood where there should have been a garden and turned over their engines. Repeatedly. Over and over, throughout the day. Bella could envisage this becoming an irritation when the summer came round and she got out a deckchair, but the situation did hold one small potential. People who stayed at home that much must know what went on in the street. They could be acquainted with the comings and goings of plumbers. So she stood on a pile of rubbish that had been there since her grandfather's day, which made it nice and stable, and looked over the garden wall.

Bella had no interest in cars other than the fact that it would have been convenient to be able to afford one, but she knew enough to recognise that this particular specimen wasn't remotely current. It looked like something out of those period dramas she never watched, was excessively noisy and currently operating well outside the spirit of every summit on world pollution. When the fumes cleared for a moment, she saw that it was sitting on somebody. "Hello," she shouted. "Hello?"

After about six "hellos" a man slid out and squinted up at her. He had brilliant blue eyes and oil splashes.

"Hello," said Bella again.

"Now then." He nodded a brief greeting.

"Are you local?" Bella asked, the tone of the "now then" making her doubtful.

"Ah'm about six foot away," he replied, "how local do you want me to be?"

"What I mean is," said Bella, "have you a knowledge of the locality?"

The man stood up and wiped his hands on a dirty rag. Even from the elevated viewpoint provided by the pile of rubbish Bella, who classed herself as tall, could see that he was several inches taller. She estimated at least five years older and further noticed, with a level of distaste, that he had elected to celebrate the sudden sunshine of a spring day by working in his vest.

"Aye, pet," he said.

Pet? Bella's distaste buds prickled even more. She'd once had a boyfriend who'd gone to Newcastle University. A boyfriend who sounded much like she did, i.e., only marginally less plummy than the Queen's Speech and who, throughout his time on Tyneside, had never gone out for the evening in shoes he couldn't run in. Geordie accents were scary. And the people who had them were not very couth. Bella had decided this after only one visit. Now it took only two flat vowels, a clause that went up at the end and a couple of "why aye pets" for her to feel really ill.

"I live in Cambridge," she said, "though just recently in this cottage, so I have local knowledge too. But not of the variety I require." In her effort to hide her distaste she sounded more like the queen than ever.

The man seemed to find this enormously funny. When he'd stopped laughing, he said, "And what variety would that be, then?"

"I need to find a plumber," said Bella, "to do a very small job at a very reasonable rate. Would you happen to know of one?"

The man reached into the car and turned off the engine. "Ah can plumb."

Bella got hold of herself. The conversation was obviously doomed to throw up all the worst in vowels, pronunciation and irritating vernacular quirks *but,* on the plus side, it could possibly save her a considerable sum of money and a lot of buggeration. "You can? I'd rather assumed that you were a motor mechanic," she said, pleasantly.

"It's all just tubes and parts," he replied, with a broad oil-ringed smile that gave him amazingly white teeth. "What d'ye want done?"

"I need a washing machine plumbed in," said Bella. "Well, not plumbed in exactly, merely attached to some taps."

"Show me."

Bella thought he'd walk round to the gate but, apparently, six-foot brick walls didn't form much of a barrier for him. Something else that her friend at Newcastle had commented upon, as she recalled.

He stood in the small scullery, virtually filling it up. A man with broad shoulders, slim hips and a peculiar tattoo which could have been some sort of Celtic rune but probably said "don't fuck with me" in Geordie. Bella inched round him and pointed to her little pile of plumbing accessories.

"You won't be able to use the sink if I do what you want," he said.

(There was the expected "ye" for "you" and "Ah" for "I" again - all destined to continue ad infinitum, ad nauseam, Bella thought.)

"I realise that," she replied. "But I have another sink in the kitchen."

"It'll look messy," he said. "And if the plughole gets

blogged, or the U-bend, it'll *be* messy."

"Look," said Bella, trying not to dwell on the use of the word "blogged" in its newly expanded sense of impeded drainage. It was a clumsy enough addition to the English lexicon as it was. "I've obviously got the bits already, but if you don't want to do the job just say so."

He studied her for a moment or two and then said, "Let me do it proper. Proper job."

"Properly," said Bella with an unconscious emphasis on the *l* and the *y*, "is apparently expensive."

"I have the gear," he said. "And I could be neighbourly and say twenty quid. How's that?" He emphasised the *l* and the *y* of neighbourly and Bella gave him a searching look and he gave her a big smile.

"It sounds as if I can't afford to say 'no.'" Which she would have really preferred on account of the tattoo and the grammar and how bright did you have to be not to flood her house? "What would it involve, exactly?"

"A morning's work and a hole or two in the wall."

"Holes in the wall?" Bella paled.

"Be fine," he said, easily. "Don't worry. My name's Harry, by the way. What's yours?"

Bella wasn't sure that she wanted to be on first-name terms with the tradesmen but he *was* her neighbour, plus there was the "don't fuck with me" rune, so she said, "I'm Bella," and held out a hand. He took it quite gently, but she'd never shaken such a hard hand in her entire life. It was a hard-worked hand. A hand that lacked delicacy and slender artistry. A hand that was designed for tightening joints and bending pipes and wielding wrenches over God knows whose head. It was also stained with oil. She didn't like it.

*****

But the plumbing she did like. Harry did it the following day with very little mess (something *he* didn't seem to like) so she was able to wash her clothes and get herself ready for the next day's visit to her professor when they would discuss any necessary adjustments to her paper before its submission to the *Philosophical Quarterly*.

She'd offered Harry a drink at one point during the plumbing proceedings. That had been around eleven o'clock in the morning and she'd produced whisky and wine. Bella came from a family that drank according to the need, not the clock. Harry said he'd rather have tea, and Bella made it in a mug and took it into the sitting room because she thought he was over the load limit for her grandmother's bentwood kitchen chairs. Used to the ascetic thinness of her professor, she found visible musculature a little ... well ... tasteless? Disturbing in some way, certainly.

"Ah'm a bit dirty for the sitting room," said Harry, who'd obviously been prepared to drink standing up in the scullery. The invitation seemed to strike him as curious. As it now did Bella, suddenly unsure of why she'd extended it.

"Oh, the sitting room is probably none too clean," she said airily. Truthfully, she had no idea whether it was or it wasn't. Dirt had been a principle in the Stone household, and Bella had been raised in the belief that there were much better things to do than go chasing after it. Her mother considered herself too creative to clean and the dailies never stayed long on account of the moodiness of the lesbian lovers and the very frank artwork about the place.

"Lot of books," remarked Harry, who didn't appear to have any desire to sit down anywhere.

In truth, there was pretty well nothing *but* books – in towering piles, half-empty crates, inelegantly stuffed bookcases and generally spread around. A veritable library without the organisational benefits of a librarian. A limited library, nevertheless. Philosophy from the ancient Greeks through Kant, Nietzsche, Hegel on to Russell, Sartre, Dennett, Scruton (to mention just the obvious) and literary works from Shakespeare through Milton all the way to Gabriel Garcia Marquez, Virginia Wolff and Salman Rushdie with the occasional erotic, some would have said pornographic, works by the likes of Anais Nin.

"Are you a reader?" Bella poured herself a whisky.

"I can read," said Harry.

Pausing, glass halfway to her lips, Bella gave him a hard look.

"But not this," he added, picking up *Physicalism, Teleology and the Miraculous Coincidence Problem*. "What do you do, for God's sake? Are you at the university?"

"Yes," said Bella, sipping her whisky. "I'm a philosophy lecturer. You could say, in fact, that I am a philosopher."

"Really," said Harry with a wide, untroubled smile. "And what's that involve then? Nothing in the vacuuming or dusting line, I notice."

*****

The next day Bella cycled to the college in some rather nice, closely fitting white jeans that had rarely been clean enough to wear before the advent of the washing machine, and an emerald green shirt that picked up the colour of her eyes. She knew that Niall would find her work stimulating and she wanted to be at her best. It was the Easter vacation so things would be quiet, and she was looking forward to a long, productive and uninterrupted afternoon.

Niall was casual in a pair of fawn cotton chinos and a pale blue shirt, no tie. His eyes gleamed as he read the paper which was, more specifically, a comparison of the opinions of Mellor and Dennett on the perception of temporal order. They disagreed on which part of the human experience facilitated an assessment of it. Mellor was of the opinion that since there is no one sensation peculiar to the perception of precedence it must therefore be the actual temporal order of the events which was significant, whereas Dennett claimed that it was the *content* of our perceptions rather than their timing which primarily allowed the determination. Bella's argument was that the two viewpoints were actually compatible. Her professor's role was to check that there were no holes in her reasoning.

Niall was ostensibly delighted with the paper, recommended a couple of ways in which she could make her argument a little clearer and then pressed her up against the desk and undid her jeans. He'd been so helpful and so smart, and he looked so overtly professorial with the sunshine from the high windows glinting off his steel grey hair that Bella didn't object when she found herself screwing around on her manuscript with its sheets peeling and flying from her bare bottom like onion skins. But she'd have preferred not to have it happen so precipitately.

Intellectual discussion was not the only foreplay she needed. She wished it were. Niall's little frowns when he pointed out her errors, his smiles when she hastily corrected herself. The urgency in both of their voices when they debated a point, and then it was up against the door or the table or the desk. Presumably it worked for some women, Bella supposed. Professors didn't persist with unviable methodologies. Plus, she had the intellect and the imagination for it so why didn't it work for her, this hot, hasty, up-against-the-filing-cabinet-type sex? And what was she going to do about it when it was only Niall who was getting hot? There was something seriously wrong with the content of her most recent perceptions and their temporal order, and it was resulting in a sub-zero score on the sexual satisfaction scale.

*****

It wasn't until Bella found "Between Internalism and Externalism in Ethics" damp and covered in plaster dust that she realised something was also wrong with the sitting room ceiling. Having studied it for a couple of uncomprehending minutes she went outside, climbed onto the pile of rubbish, settled her arms on the garden wall and watched Harry fiddling under the bonnet of yet another vintage car. A big book lay open on the front wing and Bella read a section on manifolds without understanding as much of it as she would have liked.

"So what's wrong now?" Harry asked, without looking up.

"There's water coming through the sitting room ceiling."

"It seems to me," said Harry ten minutes later, looking at the unedifying sogginess that was the bathroom floorboards, "that you could be in for a deal more than water."

"Oh God!" said Bella. "What's the cheapest thing we can do to stop it?"

"Blog up all the leaks," said Harry. "These floorboards are at least a hundred years old. If they get a chance to dry out, mebbes they'll last a bit longer."

"And the downstairs ceiling?"

"A new one."

"Couldn't I just have part of a new one?"

"I don't know what sort of plasterer is going to come and do a lash-up on a quarter of a ceiling," said Harry. "And it could still be just plaster and lath."

"Could you do one of these lash-ups? You strike me as some sort of polymath."

"I could be, if I knew what one was. "

"Having many proficiencies. In the less intellectual sense, a make do and mend person of the type produced by a peasant economy. Agricultural workers in Communist Russia, for example, were remarkably good at mending all kinds of machinery and household items. And, of necessity, sharing them."

Harry considered the ceiling for a moment or two. If he was at all interested in the versatile enterprise of bucolic

Communists, or insulted by any of the inferences that could be drawn from such a parallel, it didn't show. "Might look messy," he said.

The messy word again. Very limited vocabulary, Bella thought.

"I'll settle for its not falling on my head," she said.

*****

"You seem to live alone, Harry," she remarked, two days later.

"Aye."

"Excuse me?"

"Aye means 'yes.'"

"I realise that. I just couldn't hear you."

"That's because my head's under the bath."

Bella put the toilet lid down and sat on it. Harry had remarkably long legs, she thought. And there were muscles again. Thigh muscles were something she'd never noticed on her professor – even when his trousers were down round his ankles. Obviously he had them, otherwise he couldn't have remained standing. Which was something he seemed to prefer to do. Maybe this standing was indicative of a certain transience in their relationship? Much as one would get on a bus and, though there was a seat available at the back, decide not to bother. I'm not going far, I'll just stand. Bella didn't think that she'd mind just a short overall journey with her professor, but she'd like to have sat down occasionally.

"There," said Harry, screwing the bath panel back on.

"That should be fine now. Ah'll reseal the junction between the bath and the tiles so it won't leak when you use the shower attachment."

Bella watched him clean out old grout and fill the gap using a tube of white sealant. He had a very steady hand and carefully produced a long smooth line of thick white liquid that went on and on.

"Have you got a lover?" Bella asked when he'd got to the end and was tidying up the edge with a very effective finger.

Harry cleaned off the nozzle of the sealant gun without answering, and then he said, "Only people in books and on TV have lovers."

"So what do *you* have?" asked Bella.

"I have Mary or Jane or whatever her name happens to be."

"And have you got a Mary or Jane now?"

"No. Should we look at the sitting room ceiling again?"

*****

The *Philosophical Quarterly* had accepted Bella's paper on "The Perception of Temporal Order" and she and her professor were having a celebratory glass of champagne in college when he suddenly noticed that she was in possession of a five-litre tin of emulsion paint.

"Sitting room ceiling," Bella explained. "The trouble with having one's own house is the never-ending line of jobs to be done."

"How do you manage with that sort of thing?" Niall

asked. "Did you ever get the washing machine to work?"

"I found a proper man to do it," said Bella.

"Proper for that sort of thing," she added hastily as her professor gave her an odd look.

"Proper," he repeated. "That's an interesting word."

"Yes," said Bella. "It seems to be a workman's word. As in proper job. I suppose I've picked it up."

"I'd try not to," said her professor. "Now should we go over this crossover book proposal that you're putting together?"

"Yes, please." Bella was delighted that he'd been interested in her idea for a philosophical work on modern ethics that could appeal to both the academic and the non-academic. "And afterwards could we do it sitting down?"

"We are sitting down."

"I meant the sex."

"Oh."

So presently, Niall Grayson settled himself on the leather Chesterfield, which wasn't, perhaps, a choice spot for totally glabrous, naked haunches that were maybe planning on sweating a little, and Bella sat on top of him. Was it, she wondered, little fluxes of impatience that made him surge every now and then as if he were trying to stand up, or was he just trying to tear himself off the leather? Whatever it was, he wasn't comfortable. The surges could have been pleasurable for both of them but, in trying to help out, she'd tipped right over at one point and he'd yelled, "Oh for God's sake," so it didn't seem that they were the right sort of surges for either of them.

Bella wondered if she ought to have taken more weight on her knees. Maybe her professor just didn't have the muscle power to do controlled thrusting when she was sitting on top of him. He was an academic after all, and unlike some American academics she knew, he didn't run. Or anything. She had a weakness for academics and intellectuals but there was certainly this "or anything" about them.

There'd been that English graduate - her poet - whose foreplay, like her professor's, had been mostly sublimated into words. He'd been totally excited, totally prepared, by discussions of his own nihilistic poetry. Bella, less so. When she'd finally told him this, which she felt she could because there was not the added difficulty of a pre-existing teacher/pupil relationship, he said, "Well why did you pretend? If it had been obvious that nothing much was happening for you, I'd have done something about it. You shouldn't have faked it."

Bella didn't think she *had* faked it. She hadn't screamed aloud or bitten his shoulder or beaten the mattress with clenched fists. She'd just tried to get into the spirit of the thing rather than lying there inert, waiting for lightning to strike. How was she supposed to know that she wasn't going to come each and every time until she hadn't? Then afterwards, it had seemed churlish to mention it with the poet looking so pleased with himself. Well now she'd mentioned it. And it hadn't helped. All she'd done was create strain. The poet obviously didn't like to keep asking how she was coming along - which he was apparently unable to judge in any way at all - and she couldn't enjoy having to choreograph the entire performance, so they'd drifted apart by mutual consent.

And then there'd been that physicist. They'd had jolly discussions ranging from Newtonian determinism to the Copenhagen interpretation in quantum mechanics and whether or not the significance of the observer effect could really say anything definitive about the relevance of human consciousness to the cosmos. Including whether or not there could be a quantum dimension to the functioning of the human brain. This had all worked very well as conversational currency over meals and drinks, but then there'd been that premature ejaculation problem. Very premature, really. But not as premature as the artist who'd really just needed to paint her sat naked on a stool.

She'd had really interesting verbal exchanges with all of these men and found them sexually inarticulate. When expressed in terms of necessitating relationships, this could be represented as:

All my lovers have been thinkers.

All my lovers have been hopeless in bed.

Therefore all thinkers are hopeless in bed.

A piece of reasoning that certainly wouldn't have passed muster in the *Philosophical Quarterly* but which kept pressing in on Bella as she stared dispiritedly over Niall Grayson's head.

She didn't wonder, as a less excessively analytical woman might have done, if her failure to derive the ultimate pleasure was simply because she had never been in love with any of these men. Or even come close. In Bella's experience, love didn't have to be a factor in a necessitating relationship. Sex could perform on its own. This she had learned from an early age. And had subsequently confirmed by observing a combination of laboratory rats and electrodes whilst taking an information-gathering side trip into neuroscience. The trip hadn't helped much with her thoughts on the true nature of consciousness, but it had helped a lot with her decision not to get into bed with any more neuroscientists. She was all for scientific demystification but not to the extent of feeling like an experimental animal. "Let's get that amygdala nicely settled down," had not proved to be a stimulating battle cry. Sex as neurotransmission and love as a potpourri of neuromodulators had apparently been too much demystification. When you weren't a rat.

There'd been few demonstrations of love in the Stone household. Bella assumed that her parents loved her, but it was in a fairly abstract way - pretty much like they painted in that it wasn't always easy to see the love but it was certainly represented. They loved each other, she presumed, in that they stayed together, discussed art and literature and got along much better than a shared fleet of lesbian lovers might have led one to suppose. But Bella stayed away from the question of love because, like all philosophical questions, it was a lot easier asked than answered.

It did occur to her, however, that maybe her parents behaved the way they did because they found it impossible to get everything they needed from one person. Logically, if a man could fill all her intellectual needs but not her physical ones, then could it be correct to say that a man would be able to fulfil all her sexual needs without doing anything for her intellect? Now if this could be expressed as: if p then q ...

"Bella," said Niall Grayson, irritably. "Are you ever going to get up? My legs haven't had an effective blood supply for the past five minutes."

*****

When Harry did the sitting room ceiling he bought his own dust sheets and a length of Visqueen. He took down the damaged area, cleaned up the joists, took all the rubbish away, put up plasterboard and plastered and skimmed. All without getting a mark on the wallpaper.

"Have you ever had a long relationship?" Bella asked, as he wet the skimmer and floated it carefully over the new section, blending it into the old. Nothing he ever did was clumsy or careless, she noticed – even when the job was so small that it barely merited his concentration.

"I was married once."

"Really?"

"Aye."

"For how long?"

"Couple o' years."

"What went wrong?"

"We were young. We grew up."

"Who left who?"

"She left me."

"Why?"

"I told you. We changed. There's really no story there."

"Did you satisfy her?"

"I didn't make enough money, I don't think."

"I meant physically," said Bella, who now took double negatives in her stride.

"Eh?"

"Sexually."

Harry came down the ladder and washed off the skimmer. "Is that the sort of question philosophers go round asking?"

"We could view it academically if that would make you feel more comfortable," said Bella. "I'd really like an answer." She could see that it would open a door to the sort of discussion that Harry might not be predisposed to regard as "proper" under current circumstances, but she never allowed the few conventions she'd been brought up with to get in the way of her quest for knowledge.

"I've never answered an academic question in my life," he said. "Now, give this a few days to dry out and then you can put on that emulsion you bought."

"*I* can?"

"It's child's play. Even you'll be able to manage it."

*****

"Christ," he said a few days later. "You're hopeless. Just come down and let me do it or it'll take forever and end up all patchy."

"Here, Mr Jack-of-all-trades." Bella handed him the brush.

"Master of some," said Harry.

His interest in cars, Bella found out, had been precocious and in some way that he wasn't prepared to define, responsible for his leaving the North East for London where he'd spent some years moving from building site to building site purporting to be of whatever trade was currently in short supply.

"But they must have found out," protested Bella. "At least the men you were working alongside must've realised."

"Of course they did," said Harry. "But I was young and strong and never got sick or tired, so I fetched and carried and did all the heavy graft for them. And in return, they taught me the job. I learned as I worked. It wasn't hardly rocket science and I pick things up quickly."

Leaving construction and returning to cars had been the result of negative equity coupled with the influx of Polish builders and a chance meeting with an old man watching the start of the London to Brighton run. This meeting had precipitated the move to Cambridge and, when the old man died, Harry carried on the business in the terraced cottage that he'd been able to buy at a reasonable price because it had been a serious "fixer-upper."

"The advantage of vintage cars," he said, "is that you don't need a lot of specialist equipment like for modern electronics and there aren't many people around who can still work on old engines and gear boxes and stuff."

"A niche market," said Bella, "that only has need of agreeable neighbours."

"So why do you think I'm so helpful?"

"I hadn't really thought about it."

"There you go," said Harry. "But you would have - just about the time you were knocking on my door to complain about the noise."

"This has been copious talk for you." Bella looked thoughtfully at him. "You think if you keep talking building trades and cars I won't ask you about sexual satisfaction again?"

"A normal person wouldn't," said Harry, handing her the paintbrush. "There, finished now."

"This trade you're master of ..." she began, mischievously.

"Fifty quid including the bathroom," said Harry.

"You're very cheap." Bella handed him the cash. "Even for a noisy neighbour."

"I'm Robin Hood in reverse," said Harry. "I add on to the rich and take off from the poor."

*****

Bella felt that if she could get her professor into bed, i.e., actually into or onto a bed as opposed to the casual contact they had with more random bits of furniture, she would maybe do better. Be more relaxed. These knee tremblers were not good when executed literally. Niall, however, never visited the cottage in an organised way by arrangement. Never came for the evening or to roost. He was a man permanently in a hurry with another project always pending, and he would have to be brought into contact with a bed in passing, as it were. The guaranteed method, Bella felt, was to go upstairs herself while they were still in the academic discussion phase, take off her clothes, lie down and shout for him. He could hardly lift her bodily and lug her down to the kitchen table. If she didn't cooperate he'd never, not having Harry's foundation in hod carrying, even get her as far as the wardrobe.

So when he called in a couple of days later, ostensibly to check that she was bringing her idea for a book to a more refined point, she did what she'd planned. She was just fixing some ambient lighting to invitingly illume her nakedness in best Botticelli fashion, only slimmer, when after a sudden popping noise she was plunged into darkness.

Niall shouted up the stairs. "What the hell are you doing, Bella? All the lights have gone out down here."

Philosophers are not naturally au fait with fuse boxes, especially not old-fashioned metal jobs with an inclination to dish out electric shocks.

"For chrissakes," Niall held up the lamp from the front of Bella's bicycle, "get an electrician before you kill us both."

Bella was less frankly unsettled at the prospect of a non-lethal dose of electricity than she was at the upset of her plans to experience something soft and unavoidably horizontal with pillows. A small section of functioning circuitry was still providing light to the scullery and, having dragged her back up the cellar steps, Niall could now see that she was wearing nothing but a dressing gown. In the face of this he seemed to think that what she needed to divert her attention from her latest and frankly irritating domestic crisis was some sexual involvement with the new washing machine.

"No," said Bella, firmly removing his hands from her breasts. "Not now."

She could see from her professor's eyes that he was put out - plus there was some tense lip folding and a bit of nostril work. She knew that she might have to do the filing cabinet thing again - and more than once - before he would come back to the cottage and give her a chance to repeat the bedroom ploy. But she could accept that.

What she found a lot harder to accept was a minimum of three thousand pounds for total rewiring which would include, but not pay to make good, floorboards up everywhere and trenches the size of dry riverbeds cut into the walls. She'd called forth four separate electricians from the Local Pages to be repeatedly informed of these same depressing and seemingly unavoidable facts.

She hadn't asked for Harry's opinion because it was barely three weeks since he'd finished the bathroom leaks and the sitting room ceiling for that princely payment of fifty pounds. Bella thought about approaching her parents for the money but lately she'd been pursuing a policy of reduced contact. In casting round for a full range of possible explanations for her lack of fulfilling sexual response, she had decided that she could be repressing. Her parents having been so careless with their own sex lives, leaving them around the place for anybody to discover (making her girlfriends hysterically giggly and her boyfriends insanely optimistic), Bella knew that it didn't take much of a grounding in Freud to work out that she must have quite a bit to repress when it came to fornicating on furniture. Including the fact that she could be a lesbian. She hoped not. Lesbianism she could accept in principle, but having more lesbians wailing round the kitchen table and maybe having strange rebound affairs with Harry she simply couldn't face. Prospective lesbianism aside, she didn't want to do more repressing than she was already doing – and certainly not three and a half thousand pounds' worth.

*****

"Harry," she called, "were you ever an electrician on those building sites? Do you understand electricity?"

"I wouldn't say I understood it," he called back, from under a car. "But I can make it go round a house and come out at the light sockets and wall plugs without killing anybody."

"But this," he said an hour later, "is an absolute bloody mess. The fuse box is live. All of the wires in the landing light switches are live. Even the earths. The place can't have been rewired *properly* since it was changed over from gas. Or candles. It's just been messed with and re-messed with on the inspired botching system. It's almost impossible to work out what's going on. It'll have to be completely redone. Those electricians weren't lying to you, pet."

"You've got the hang of adverbs," Bella sighed. "Is there no way you can extend beyond that to these electrical circuits?"

"Almost impossible."

"The same way I feel about trying to raise three thousand pounds."

"You'll need a new fuse box whatever happens. That's a hundred up front at least."

"I can manage that. But I can't live by candles and torches. I need my computer. Please try."

"*Okay*. I'll get my circuit tester. But ah'm not promisin' anything."

*****

"Harry?"

"Aye?"

"Have you got another Mary Jane yet?"

"Nah. So much of my time is spent repairing your house."

"Right, then," said Bella. "I can see that you wouldn't want to talk about your ex-wife, but could we discuss a hypothetical Mary Jane?"

"You mean a Mary Jane that doesn't exist?"

"Exactly," agreed Bella. "Now, does she have orgasms?"

"Didn't you ever get a book? You seem to have books on everything else."

"I want a man's point of view."

"And men don't write books?"

"I want an ordinary man. Unedited man. The experience of any old Joe. Or Harry."

"We're going to have to have this discussion, are we?"

"If you ever want to get out of the loft space," said Bella. "Remember, the bolt is on the outside of the trapdoor and

I'm the lady with the lamp."

"Well hold it up a bit, will ye?"

"Orgasms," said Bella firmly. "Yes or no?"

"With me there or without me there?"

"With you, of course. Stop being evasive."

"Just trying to get things clear. I can see this is going to be a deeply philosophical discussion and I don't want to get lost off."

"To be clear, then. Does Mary Jane have an orgasm when she has sex with you?"

"Sex or just sex?"

"So you've got a nascent grasp on semantics," said Bella irritably, "in which case you'd better define your terms."

"I don't think I'll bother," said Harry. "I'll just say that now I'm fully growed the answer is 'yes.'"

"*Growed?* **Growed?**"

Harry squinted into the beam of the inspection lamp. "*Grown*," he said. "Matured. Including mentally."

"How can you be sure?" asked Bella.

"Well," said Harry, "I swear less. I don't punch people anymore and I stopped nicking things."

"About the orgasm," said Bella crossly. "How can you be sure about the orgasm?"

"Oh, that. Yeah, well … It depends on what sort of sex we're having."

"You mean sex or just sex?"

"No. I mean whether or not I can be sure."

"Listen," said Bella, dangerously. "It's supposed to be *you* that gets lost off in discussions with *me*! Tell me exactly under which sexual circumstances you can be certain that Mary Jane has an orgasm, isn't faking, and how you can be certain."

"I can't," said Harry. "I just can't …"

"Can't tell me or just can't tell?"

"Can't see where on earth this cable is coming from."

"Orgasms," said Bella, warningly.

"I'm not sure how I can put this exactly …"

"Anatomically?"

"Without drilling another hole in your ceiling."

"Harry!" Getting shrill with impatience.

"*What?*"

"Why won't you just say it? Can't you think of enough euphemisms?"

"Aye, that could be it. But also ah'm dying of heat stroke in this friggin' loft and I need to think about wiring. Have you got any cold beer?"

"I don't drink beer."

"Here then." Harry fished in a pocket and gave her his door keys. "Get me a one out of my fridge, will ye?"

"A one? *A* one?"

"Aye. That's right. Two."

Harry's cottage was exactly like Bella's in design but there the similarities ended. The inside of the fridge, for instance, was quite different. It contained food - not all of it pre-packaged - and there was a noticeable absence of green mould. The draining board and the sink were totally clear of dishes and carefully wiped. The waste bin was not full to overflowing or surrounded by empty wine bottles.

The bed sheets, and Bella was as astonished to find herself looking at them as Harry would have been could he have seen her, were clean and the pillowcases showed signs of having been ironed. In the sitting room, there was only one bookshelf and it was full of antique leather-bound books on motor engineering.

"You realise," said Bella, as she handed him the beer, "that in keeping your house like that you run the risk of destroying a perfectly good social stereotype?"

"Unlike you," said Harry, "who just confirms the impression that those loud-mouthed, self-righteous, slobby students at demonstrations turn into messy, opinionated, nosey smart-alecs who are apparently useless for most practical purposes."

"I was evidently mistaken," snapped Bella. "Stereotype confirmed. That tattoo does mean 'don't fuck with me,' doesn't it?"

"No," said Harry, getting back into the loft. "The tattoo is just a pretty picture - which is more than can be said for the one you've been trying to get me to paint for the past hour. Why don't you ask that old man who comes here to answer your questions for you?"

"That old man, as you put it, is my philosophy professor," Bella shouted after him.

"Stereotype confirmed," Harry shouted back. "Useless for all practical purposes."

It was Bella who felt most strongly that her character had been besmirched by this conversation. Harry continued to work as if no significant words had been exchanged. Possibly, that was another advantage gained from grafting on endless building sites - a Teflon-coated sense of self that did not anguish over other people's opinions of him. He could make old cars - and electricity, it turned out - run again. He did not need peer reviewed papers to validate either himself or his existence.

*****

Bella thought about this occasionally as she prepared a new and foolproof plan for luring her professor into/onto an actual bed.

When she finally put the plan into action, she was rewarded with a new and illuminating thought on the subject of time: it's surprising how long it can last when a woman is lying on a bed waiting not to have an orgasm. Bella had persuaded herself that it was the limitation of location that had handicapped Niall Grayson because, she reasoned, there were some things that years spent exercising nothing but brain synapses just couldn't work against. Gravity being one of them. But now she had Niall on an actual bed where everything could articulate without having to work too hard against natural forces, and still he was operating as if time - even this curious temporal hiatus that she seemed to be experiencing - was of the essence. And technique one of those things that had never needed a peer review.

Maybe he was a sort of Descartes, Bella thought. A Descartes in reverse -in that if he didn't think about something then it wasn't there. If his mental list of erogenous zones didn't extend past nipples first, nipples second and nipples third, then quite plainly there was nothing else in his reality except nipples. And if he hadn't expanded his reality in forty-five years and over a quarter of a century of sexual activity, it clearly wasn't going to happen now. Like those experimental kittens that were reared in an environment where there were only horizontal planes, and were forever afterwards apparently unable to relate to vertical ones, Niall Grayson, reared in an era of page three girls, might never get past the idea that foreplay could consist of anything other than breasts. At least not without a serious talking-to. And Bella had done serious talking with her poet, a much younger and more impressionable mind, and it hadn't worked. So she couldn't see re-educating a man who ought to have learnt a lot better by now.

How could Professor Grayson be so brilliant at picking holes in her reasoning and so painfully oblivious to her somewhat less than subtle sexual cues? And how could she ever know if she could ring the bell on the orgasm scale if she'd never had a lover who was remotely thorough?

*****

"Harry, would you have sex with me?"

No verbal foreplay, just straight to the point.

"Eh?" Startled, Harry bumped his head on an open car bonnet as he swung round.

"Would you have sex with me?" Clear and sharp without any hint of normal - even expected - awkwardness.

227

She might have been asking a waiter to bring her a clean glass.

Harry glanced from her to the garden walls. "Shout a bit louder," he said. "There's probably somebody at the end of the street who hasn't heard."

"I doubt they're listening," said Bella.

"You've never lived in a street before, have you?"

"Not where people concrete over their lawns and mend cars on them. No, I haven't," replied Bella crossly, nodding at the two cars that now occupied her garden as part of the "please mend my electricity" transaction. Plus, this bizarre working-class prudery wasn't the response she'd been looking for. A touch of enthusiasm – even gratitude – wouldn't have come amiss.

"Pet," said Harry, rubbing his head, "that university is full of male students who must be falling over themselves to get to you. You could do a proper practical survey on … what is it? Physical, Tele-something-or-other and the Curious Orgasm Problem. Might even get into that philosophy magazine thing."

"Are you trying to be funny?"

"Just wondering why you're coming to me when you must have your pick of a crowded field. I mean, the only time you come to me is when stuff isn't working right and you want it fixed."

For the first time in her life, Bella turned red.

"Oh," said Harry.

But if there was one thing that Bella's upbringing had given her, it was the ability to remain poised under all circumstances, so it was only seconds before she recovered.

"Well then," she said. "Are you up for it?"

"No need to make it sound so romantic."

She gave him a glare.

"Just be direct," he said. "That's your thing. Is it because you can't afford to have the job done properly?"

"I *want* the job done properly," said Bella. "And I wasn't planning on paying you anything."

"Ah'm relieved about that."

"*Stop it.* Yes or no?"

"Rule number one in my world - when you're offered a job, at least have the decency to show up."

"Could we do it now?"

"No."

"Is the owner in a hurry for the car?"

"No."

"So why not now?"

"For the same reason I wouldn't re-varnish this dashboard now. The atmosphere's not right."

"I see." Bella was put out.

"My grandfather was a craftsman," said Harry. "Not my father - he was a car thief who did a stretch for not listening when Grandpappy said, as he frequently did: 'If a job's worth doing, it's worth doing well.' Okay?"

"Fine," said Bella with an exaggerated sigh. "I'll leave it to you."

But she knew she shouldn't. It was obvious what Harry meant. He thought she needed romancing. Flowers, restaurants and stuff. He thought a courtship ritual was going to be necessary to get her psychologically prepared. But that was the last thing she wanted. She could already see him in a clean shirt, stiffly delivering a bunch of shocking pink carnations and some badly chosen wine. Booking a meal at the Star of India or some pseudo-French place and picking her up with his hair slicked back and a dreadful shiny suit in which she'd be catching her reflection for the rest of the evening. There'd be painful conversation with him saying "eh" all the time, and delivering terrible little homilies about "Grandpappy" or the plots of D.C. Comics movies. So now she desperately wished that she hadn't left it to Harry because he was going to ruin everything with an overzealous inclination to "do it proper."

And it would all begin the very next time she saw him. Even before the hideous "*date*," as she was sure he'd call it. In his efforts to charm, he'd lose all the natural charm he possessed (which, she reflected in annoyance, was as appealing as it was unaccountable) and replace it with some heavy, oozy, sticky variety, ludicrously laced with winks and lead-weighted Geordie witticisms. She could have to bear all of that and when they got back to the cottage he might do nothing more impressive than say, "Now pet, why don't you just come over here and sit on my face?"

It was quite clear that the only possible course of action – for both of their sakes and, most especially, for the sake of her next house catastrophe – was to tell him, the very next morning before he could say one word, that she had made a silly mistake in a fit of pique with her professor and could they both just forget it?

*****

Bella's idea for a book needed to be assembled into a synopsis, as the aforementioned professor had requested. And she had to get on with it. But instead she spent the rest of the day (during which she didn't have to go into college) in a state of ridiculous anxiety lest the new embarrassing caricature of Harry begin its charm offensive before an acceptable period of reflection would allow her to decently abort it. Normally, she had a mind that could slough off spurious thoughts, intrusive emotions, even pain, in the pursuit of academic excellence, but just now she couldn't get rid of the shameful idea that "Come here and sit on my face, pet" wasn't quite the turnoff it ought to have been.

Finally, after making some sporadic and not very impressive notes, she decided to have another glass of wine - she'd already had two - in order to ensure a good night's sleep devoid of the sort of tossing and turning that might lead to an insidious change of heart.

It was well past midnight when she came awake, enjoying the pleasant sensation of being gently held against a large, warm body.

"Don't scream, pet. It's just me."

"Harry! What on earth are you doing here?"

She wasn't normally prone to superfluous questions. He

let her pull back, saying nothing.

"*Harry.*"

"I thought I'd had yet another request to fix something, and I have to fit these things in when I can."

She could hear the smile in his voice.

"But how did you get into the house?"

"Oh, aye. Well, that's just another of those things I happen to have picked up. Nothing you'd want to mention on a CV, though. Just another casual skill."

"I'd have had a bath if I'd known you were coming," said Bella, indignant now.

"I had a shower," said Harry. "If that makes you feel better."

She could hear that he was smiling again.

"So," he went on, "do you want to have grubby but safe sex with a nascent cat burglar?"

"You pick up words quickly." Bella still sounded sniffy.

"Aye."

"But you won't do *it* quickly, will you?"

"If you still want it done, I'll do it at the right pace for the job."

"Sometimes, you know, you're just infuriating. Honestly, I could punch you."

"Go ahead," said Harry, "if that's how you want to start. I'd prefer a kiss but it's never been said that I can't take a punch."

Bella sighed. "I really, really didn't see this one coming."

"And you really, *really* don't like being second-guessed, do you?"

"No," Bella sighed, moving closer again, "but oddly enough it's starting to feel rather pleasant."

*****

Several hours later she woke from an engulfing but very brief sleep to see Harry pulling on his jeans in the light of dawn.

"Can we do this again?" she asked.

"We've already done it three times."

"I know. And to think that somebody whose name temporarily eludes me said that in every great work there is only one climax."

Harry smiled at her.

"So, when *can* we do this again?" she asked.

He sat on the edge of the bed and picked up her hand. "No point to keep fixing something that's not broke," he said. "You just need to find yourself a man who can be bothered to read the instruction manual."

"But that's the point," said Bella. "No one can cover it from start to finish. It's not going to be possible to find a man who can satisfy me in every conceivable way. A person has so many different requirements – emotional, intellectual, aesthetic, physical. It's simply not realistic to expect any one man to ..."

Harry listened to her go on in this vein for a few more minutes and then he said: "You see, pet, that's why you're the philosopher and ah'm the plumber. I can't get my head round that."

"Well it's simple enough," said Bella, irritably. "Maybe

I'm not explaining it clearly."

"You're explaining it a lot, though."

"Then you should have understood it by now, surely?"

"I didn't say I couldn't *understand* it," Harry pointed out. "What I meant was, I'm just dumb enough to believe that I should be able to have sex with the same woman I go to the vintage car rallies with. And the *Avengers* movies. And then to see dogs at Crufts or flowers at Chelsea ... whatever it is that she wants to do. And have both of us enjoy it all. Simply because we're in each other's company. I think they call it love. I don't know what philosophers call it, of course."

Silently, Bella watched him pull on his T-shirt. In the bedroom doorway he turned and said: "By the way, as I was - er - coming in last night, I noticed the bottom sash of the kitchen window is rotten. Ah'll make you a replacement if you like."

"So you're a carpenter now?"

"Not really. Carpentry takes more practice then ah've had. So it won't be a proper job."

"Thank God for that," said Bella. "I'm not quite clear on the price I could end up paying for this one, yet."

GYPSY

"Give it another chance? he says, purple in the face. This is the chief dog trainer, you understand, and she's just a corporal. Give it another chance? The hell 1 will. The dog has failed and that's the end of it. It's too nervy for this business. It'll get somebody killed. It's not nervy, she says, as cool as you like, just sensitive. Well, I thought he was going to explode on the spot. *Sensitive*, he shouts, *sensitive?* This is the bloody army. It's not allowed to be sensitive. The only sensitivity round here is on the trigger of the SA80. But she's not to be intimidated. I'd like to explain, she says. So explain, he says - which surprised me, I must say - explain to me the difference between nerves and sensitivity in a dog. Well, she says, after a second or two, it's like the difference between men and women. Men think and women think, but women are thoughtful. That's the difference.

"Not getting it, he says. Too touchy-feely for me. All I see is a nervy dog that will get somebody blown to hell. Put it away and get the next one. *Now*. That's an order, Corporal. She went off then and he comes up to me and says: I don't know, Sergeant. These women are good dog trainers but they're under the impression that dogs are like children - have to be given a chance at the school sports even when they can't run worth a toss. And I have to explain to them that these are dogs, and we must give them every chance we can, but not when it comes to people's lives.

"He understood her feelings, of course. We both did. Half the dogs that come to us are at the end of the road. They've been most every place else and nobody wants them. If they fail with us, that's it, there's nowhere else to go. Women take things harder, Chief, I said, they're different."

"As the government will find to its cost if it makes them teeth arm," added the engineer officer. "Actually, it will be to our cost."

"That's just what the chief said to me: they'll be the death of us one way or another, Sergeant, mark my words. Don't get me wrong though, he goes on. I would be prepared to die for a woman, especially one that looked like Corporal Connolly, but I'm buggered if I'm going to die for her bloody dog."

The conversation stopped then because the operating theatre door opened. The sergeant jumped up anxiously, but the orderly shook his head. "Not yet."

"Here," the engineer offered a packet, "have a smoke."

"No," said the sergeant. "Thanks, but I don't. I could murder a whisky, though."

"Sorry," said the engineer. "No can do. But this dog,

then. It must have got another chance or it wouldn't have been out here in the first place."

"It did," said the sergeant. "But it was a funny thing. We had all the mine detection dogs lined up for the draft and as good a lot as you'd find anywhere in the world. Better. Then disaster. Big parvovirus outbreak. Of course they'd all been vaccinated, so this was the unusual bit - there'd been some sort of vaccine breakdown. I don't understand the science of it, but there we were with fifty per cent of them on their backs with their legs in the air, looking like their time had come. So sort out some more, says the commandant, furious. We haven't got any more, sir, says the chief. The next lot aren't quite ready. I can't imagine … So get back down the friggin' dog school and imagine again, shouts the commandant. Of course he was just sounding off, he knew we couldn't send half-trained dogs, but the chief and me went back and started reassessing some of the failures. And that's how Corporal Connolly's dog got a second chance. Then the draft was delayed - nothing to do with us - and the vets had been flogging away with twenty-four-hour IV drips and whatnot, and finally we were okay. But Annie Connolly, she had volunteered to come here to clear mines and she wanted to use that damned dog anyway. It's going to be my life at risk, she says to the chief, so I'd like to decide which dog's paws to put it in. Then take it, he says, but don't come crying back to me when the bloody thing gets you killed."

"Women, eh?" said the engineer.

"Amazin'," said the sergeant with a sigh. "I'll never

understand them. God alone knows why Connolly had such a thing about that dog. Why she liked it more than any of the others. Nobody else could see anything to it at all. And maybe that's why Connolly did. Like it was an abandoned child. We didn't even know where it had come from. Just found it one day, all skin and bones, tied to the camp gate with a note round its neck like Paddington Bear. 'Please look after this dog.' There'd been gypsies in the area and we thought it might have been theirs, so that's what we called it. Gypsy. It was a bit of a collie, with blue merle coat colouring and one wall-eye and one brown one. Oddest thing to look at. And nervy, like the chief said. I never thought it would shape up at anything, let alone mine detection. You need something altogether, well ..." He paused.

"What?" asked the engineer.

"More easily persuaded to sit still as a statue and stare fixedly at the dirt over a mine for as long as it takes. In training we have to use a big scam that some dogs are just too bright to buy into. Sooner or later, they get fidgety feelings of being duped."

"Dangerous," said the engineer.

"Very."

"Is that what happened here?"

"God knows," said the sergeant. "We just got a signal to say they'd found Corporal Connolly and then it was: here's a veterinary officer, a tranquilliser gun and a helicopter and don't come back without that dog."

The operating theatre door opened again and the

sergeant jumped to his feet. "Doctor? Colonel, sir, any news?"

The RAMC surgeon was worn out. "She'll live, Sergeant," he said. "She'll have problems, but she'll cope. Won't be clearing any more minefields but ... well ... there we are." He paused to let the news sink in, then: "That dog though, wasn't that really something? Do they award medals to dogs? It was all she talked about whenever she was conscious. Not a dry eye in the whole field ambulance. Including mine. Press can't wait to interview her, get a photo opportunity with the dog. But how on earth does an animal accomplish something like that, Sergeant? It was so calm, she said. It just sat there waiting, and then when she was able to make an effort, it got up and started to walk. Of course, she couldn't stand because her balance had gone, as had her hearing. Not to mention the blood loss, the shrapnel wounds, night coming on and the thermometer dropping like a stone along with her body temperature. She dragged herself after it, inch by inch, she said, while it kept just in front where she could feel its tail. Inch by inch for hour after hour through a pitch-black minefield to get within reach of a patrol. They picked her up at dawn, but the dog had gone by then. She was just holding its harness. God, I hope you find it."

"Sir," began the sergeant, but the surgeon wasn't finished. "Seems odd though, doesn't it?" he went on. "To leave her at the end like that? And the harness was still buckled, you know. In her hand, the patrol said, still buckled. And she was unconscious."

"Sir," began the sergeant again. "I'm sorry, sir, but the dog is dead."

"Oh, Christ, no! You found its body?"

"What was left of it, sir. We could see it below us. In the minefield."

"Oh, Christ! What a terrible shame! Why are there never any real happy endings? Why the hell would it wander back into the minefield?"

"Well, to be honest, sir," said the sergeant, "we assumed that it had never left."

"But it brought her out of there," said the surgeon, surprised. "Corporal Connolly might be a bit deaf - pretty deaf at the moment - but she's fully compus mentis. And you and I both know she wasn't getting out of there on her own."

*****

"Corporal Connolly! Annie." He had to shout.

"Sergeant?"

"Who's the lucky one then? The surgeon says you're going to be fine."

"Yes."

"But. Annie …"

"Yes?"

"About the press, Annie, and the story they're wanting to write about Gypsy."

"Yes, Sarge."

"It's just that …"

"She's dead," finished Corporal Connolly, looking up

with clear and focused eyes. "I understand … She didn't set it off, you know … The mine. It was something falling from a Chinook during that surprise skirmish. But she looked so beautiful, Sarge. Like she'd just had a bath. All brushed and silky. Ready for Crufts. Ready to take the 'best in show.' Step by step, she went. Me barely moving. Barely hanging in there. I was scared, Sarge, so bloody scared … I …"

"I know, Annie. I know." He laid a careful hand on her arm.

"It was black dark. I didn't know south from north, up from down. I thought it was going to last forever, the pain, the nausea, the fear … Eventually, she just sat down - at the road, you see. Just sat and waited. Looking at me. Smiling at me. You know how they can, that little thing they do with their noses and their lips wrinkle up? Little apologies really. So sweet. I rolled over after a bit so I could touch her and, you know, when I did there was no more pain … no more fear. And then the patrol was there and they picked me up, and all I had left was a harness."

Corporal Connolly started to cry then, harsh sobs, and the sergeant said, "You rest, Annie. This is too hard for you just now. Tomorrow, the next day, we'll get the story straight. You'll feel better then."

"Sarge." She got the sobs under control.

"Yes?"

"I might feel better but the story will be the same. Always the same."

The sergeant put his beret back on. "Look, Annie …"

"I know, Sarge, and I know she's dead. She went up in the initial explosion. She was dead all along."

*****

"Looks just like a harness to me," said the engineer curiously as the sergeant, picking it up from the pre-op room, went very pale.

"Just like the harness I watched Corporal Connolly cut the buckles off and throw in the incinerator six months ago when the dog failed its pass-out," said the sergeant, quietly. "And nothing like the harness the dog set out in yesterday morning."

He turned the thing over in his hands and through the bloodstains on the green army webbing the engineer could pick out some lettering in black felt-tip. It read: Gypsy - donor unknown.

"Annie was crying," went on the sergeant, "as she watched it burn. I tried to say some stuff about the dog. You know … You can't win them all, you can't take them all home, stuff like that. But she wasn't having it. She grabs my arm and says: Gypsy has to have another chance, Gypsy has to have another chance, over and over. It's not going to happen, I says finally. And you've got to stop this, Corporal. Right now. This is your job and you can't do it like this. You've been in this situation before and you know how it works. What's so damned different about this one? She looks a little surprised then, as if she's just realised she's been running on a bit, and then she says, quite calmly: I don't know, Sarge. It's just something in the way she looks at me. When the chips are down, she'll deliver. Get the job done. Somehow."

ACKNOWLEGEMENTS

As always I owe a tremendous debt to my husband Andrew for helping me prepare this collection for formatting by Jason and his team at Polgarus Studio.

I also owe to Andrew my twenty-two years as an army wife which, if nothing else, gave me the background to write a couple of these stories. Most specifically, the story "Gypsy" which is dedicated to the men, women and animals of the Royal Army Veterinary Corps whose need for tremendous but often lonely courage so frequently passes unsung.

I must also thank our son Max for designing and preparing the cover, and our niece Dr Rebecca Roache PhD whose paper on the perception of time I purloined and summarised, no doubt inaccurately, in order to create a believable background for the entirely fictitious character of Isabella Stone.

P.S. In accordance with the rules of this newly "woke" world I make the following statement: I'm allowed to satirise Geordies because I am one.

Lightning Source UK Ltd.
Milton Keynes UK
UKHW021110100521
383424UK00004B/82